Heir to the Throne

Children of the Wild, Volume 7

Prudence MacLeod

Published by Prudence MacLeod, 2024.

Heir to the Throne
by
Prudence MacLeod
(second edition)
Copyright February 24 / 2018

HEIR TO THE THRONE

First edition. March 8, 2024.

Copyright © 2024 Prudence MacLeod.

ISBN: 978-1927478714

Written by Prudence MacLeod.

After the destruction

The carnage had been beyond description, beyond belief, beyond imagining. The three vampires kicked in the door of the church, bringing a madness, a hell, none of the people could have imagined. Two of the beasts tore into the gathered families, ripping and tearing at them. Blood and bodies were everywhere.

Those who tried to escape were seized by the third vampire and tossed back into the room to be killed and fed on by the others. The scar-faced man laughed in mad delight as his creations mangled and destroyed the gathered people there, their tortured screams music to his ears.

When it was done, or it seemed to be so, he attacked and killed the other two vampires. "There is only one god," he said, "and I am that one true god." He tore the heads from the vampires and threw them out the window, then set fire to the church.

As the flames leaped up, a small boy who'd hidden under the altar, noticed movement. One man was still alive. Terrified, the boy nonetheless went to him and dragged him out from under the bodies. "That way," gasped the man as he tried to point. The child understood and together they made their way out of the burning building. The mad vampire was gone.

Darkness had fallen before the boy managed to get the injured man to his home. Only then did the child break down and weep, crying out his anguish for his mother and father, his sisters, all of whom had died in the attack.

While the boy wept, the man struggled to bind his own wounds. He had also lost his family in that church of blood, his wife and son tortured and killed before his eyes. As the boy wept and cried pitifully for his mother, Melosh bandaged his own wounds and, pushing down his grief and sorrow, vowed vengeance. He would find a way to kill the demons, and then he would hunt them.

Returning to the boy, he took him into his arms to comfort him. "Hush now. You are Johan, yes? We will learn, study together, and we will hunt them, you and I, Johan. We will hunt and destroy the beasts, torture them as they tortured our families, then kill them, destroy them utterly. For now, we must leave this place. I know where to go, where we can hide, learn, and grow strong, you and I."

He carried the child outside and tucked him into his old car. This village was no longer safe. Two days later they arrived at a rundown cottage that had once been the gate house for a nobleman's mansion. The Bolsheviks had burned the manor house long ago, but the cottage remained.

THE FIRST DAYS AT THE cottage were difficult for Melosh. Even though he and his wife had three children, he had taken little interest in their care. Now he had to care for the child that had saved him from the fire, and he had no idea what to do for him. Both man and boy were numbed by what had happened, what they'd suffered, what they'd witnessed.

The place was damp and moldy after several years of being uninhabited. As they struggled to clean it and make it more livable, they found several of the old man's books. The most dog-eared volume was called The Vampire Hunter. Holding it in his hand as though a priceless treasure, Melosh gazed at the faded cover for a long time, then he set it aside. He planned to study it in detail later.

Melosh's grandfather had lived in that cottage for many years, and often spoke of the wealth his master had buried before the Bolsheviks had come. It took Melosh and Johan eight years to find it, but find it they did. That gave them the financial means to continue the vendetta, the hunt for vampires.

They studied books, combat arts, weapons, medieval torture methods, plus any and all monster lore they could find. The boy grew into a man, a man with a burning rage inside, a deep desire to avenge his mother, and a silent, secret, hatred for Melosh, the man who forced him to remember, the man who would not let him forget his mother's screams. Melosh fed that rage in him, nurtured it, drove it, for it matched his own.

He would often find the boy outside, gazing up at the night sky. "Johan?"

"Mother used to love looking at the stars. She would catch me watching her when I was supposed to be sleeping, and she would quietly call me out beside her. I'd crawl up into her lap and star gaze with her. I sometimes come out here and look at the stars to remember."

"Yes, remember, but remember the last moments of her life, Johan. Never forget that. No mother is safe while that thing lives. Remember that. We must find and kill it. Remember her screams."

The boy, nearly a man now, turned and grabbed the older man by the collar, shaking him. "You think I don't remember? You think I don't hear her screams, feel her terror, see her step between me and the monster? Every moment of every day, I hear those screams."

He thrust the older man away. "Sometimes I just want to remember her gentleness, her smile, the touch of her hand. Tell me you don't feel the same for your wife."

"I do, Johan, I do. She, too, enjoyed the stars on a summer's night. That is why I'm so determined to kill this thing, to make the night safe for all mothers and wives to enjoy."

"We will avenge them, Melosh. We will slay that monster and then they can rest peacefully. On that day I will join my mother in that world beyond."

"You mean heaven? You would kill yourself?"

"Da. This is no life, Melosh. Heaven? I don't believe in that place, only hell. I believe in that one because I've been there. No, we will kill the monsters, then leave this world to the people. This is no place for monsters."

"So, you think we're monsters now?"

"Are we not? After what we've done, after what we plan to do? What else have we become?" With that the young man stood and went back inside, to his bed, to blessed sleep, the only place he could find relief from the bloody images in his mind, and he hated Melosh for constantly reminding him.

Up to that point they had only hunted and captured animals, large animals, bears, elk, and tortured them as they learned and practiced how to confine and control large powerful creatures. The next day they planned to hunt a man, a man who had beaten his wife to death, a man the entire small town hated and feared.

They found him and took him down with tranquilizer darts, just as they'd practiced. The man awakened slowly as the drug wore off. Suddenly terrified, he began to struggle, but his movements cause incredible pain, so he lay still whimpering. A young man approached, and he tried to plead with him, but a large ball gag in his mouth prevented speech.

"You are awake now, I see. Do not struggle, for the wire will cause you great pain. Ah, what does it matter, I will cause you great pain anyway." He grabbed the wire that confined the man and twisted it tighter, eliciting a scream.

"Hurts, doesn't it? It might interest you to know I sat outside your house listening to your wife scream, twice. Sadly, I was not there to prevent her death." He bent closer to stare into the man's eyes. "There is no one here to prevent your death at my hands either. Just as your wife saw her death in your eyes, now you see your own death in mine." The captive screamed again as the wire was tightened once more, then the young man walked away.

They stood together as they finished burying the man's body. The younger man was quiet, gazing at the fresh dirt. "It was only just that he die, Johan, pay for his crime, his brutality against the weak."

"I know, but was it necessary to torture him?"

"It was a learning experience. As he paid for his cruelty, he helped us in our holy quest, taught us how to bring the screams from the vampire when we catch him. At the end, he finally did something good for his fellow man."

"Holy quest, Melosh? Holy? No, there is nothing holy about what we do, what we have become."

"We do what we must so the rest of the people will not know what we know, will not suffer as we suffered. We do what we must to learn the things we need to know, so we can protect the weak."

"Protect the weak? Is that why we do what we do, truly?"

"That is part of it, yes, but we do it to bring justice as well. That and we are preparing ourselves for the ultimate battle. Johan, you know what we will face. Save your pity for those who deserve it, not scum like this one was, or monsters like the vampire. Scum like this one will serve our needs as we learn what we need to know for the final battle with the beast."

Johan just nodded then took up his shovel and walked back toward the car. Melosh clapped a gentle hand on his shoulder. "Tomorrow we leave this place. We will go to St. Petersburg, find a place to work and train, then begin our search for recruits. We cannot do this alone; against the vampire we will need help."

For the next twenty years they recruited and trained true believers, developed a network of hunters that stretched out over much of Europe. In all that time they studied, trained, and eliminated a number of hardened criminals, cruel and savage men. Yet, in all that time they never once encountered a true vampire.

Forewarned

With a gasp, the queen of the vampires sat up in the bed, holding her hand on her breast as she dragged deep breaths into her lungs. The king was instantly awake and had her in his arms. "Sally, breathe girl, breathe, I've got you. You're safe now, I've got you."

She melted against him, clinging tightly to him. "Oh god, Harald, there are times when this ability of mine scares me."

"Perhaps it was only a dream, my love, a nightmare and nothing more."

"No, it was a forewarning, I can tell the difference."

"What did you see?"

"It was Lady Hawk, but a side of her we haven't seen before. She was cold, hard as stone, without compassion or pity. I couldn't tell what was going on, but I heard Victor ask her, 'What of these men, do we kill them too?'

"Harald, she answered with a single word, but she was so cold and dispassionate that it terrified me. My love, she will become queen. Somehow we have to make sure she becomes a queen we would want for our people."

"I agree, but what you saw doesn't scare me so much, as I've had to make such decisions before. It's never an easy command to give, and you have to be hard, or it will destroy you. The battle in Scotland where we rescued the werewolves was an example. I had no other option, I had to protect my own people.

"I do agree with you, though, we need to guide Ronni as she comes into her own as a leader."

"How's the mentoring going?"

He chuckled at that. "I think I'm scaring her. She seems to like it, but I know she's puzzled as to why I'm suddenly taking such an interest. Maybe you should talk to her."

"Me?"

"You, my love. What do you think, take her into our confidence? Tell her what you've seen?"

"Would that be wise? Tell me honestly, do you think she can handle that, or will it go to her head?"

"I think it will scare the daylights out of her." He chuckled at the thought. "No, love, I get no sense at all that she would become a spoiled little princess. The past couple of years have given her many opportunities for just that, especially the way Igor and the wolves dote on her, but she's remained true, a hard working, and full member of our community.

"Yes, she's full of mischief much of the time, but that fun-loving nature is tempered with a sense of loyalty and duty. I think she can handle it."

"Are you considering making her the heir now, or leaving it for a future date?"

The king sighed and hugged her gently. "No love, I think sooner is better, both for the monarchy and for Rhonda. However, first I have to gain the support of her future advisors, of as many of our people as I can. Both Ella and Gudrun are strong candidates, and more natural choices, for the title and the job."

"Sadly, that won't happen, Harald. Oh, I could be completely wrong about this, but ..."

"No, sweet Sally, I won't bet against you on this one. No, your visions make it abundantly clear, the Lady Hawk will succeed me as monarch. All that remains now is to bring the others onside, and then convince Ronni to accept the role."

WHILE THE KING AND queen discussed a future Rhonda wouldn't want, she was conferring with her best friend, Clara, as they worked side by side in the lab. "I'll confess, Clara, I like Harald being the big brother for me, but as much as I like it, I think he's up to something."

"Oh? Like what?"

"I have no idea at all, but it's starting to feel like school."

"School?"

"Yeah, he says stuff like, "We've got to send an agent out to Seattle to check out those rumors. Who do you think should go, Ronni?" Then he tells me where the other teams are, who's available, and after I make a suggestion he asks why that agent. I tell him, we discuss it a bit, then he sends the one I suggested. Right now we've got Marlene in Vancouver, and he shows me every report."

"Uh-oh."

"What? What uh-oh? What do you mean, uh-oh? Clara, talk to me."

"Well, neither of us was raised in a monarchy but, with so many long-lived people around, why would a king turn to a younger person for advice and to confer?"

"I have no idea at all. Come on, tell me what you think is going on?"

"Sounds to me like he's training you to take over his job."

"What???"

"Think about it. This is a monarchy, Harald's the king. Now, Ella made him king because she didn't want the job. A monarchy needs to have an heir ready to step in should anything happen to the current monarch. It provides stability to the social structure."

"Okay, fine, do you honestly think he's trying to groom me for the job?"

"Looks like it to me, honey."

"No way, I don't want that. I don't. What about Gudrun? She'd be perfect, a natural leader, centuries of experience, and more. Then there's Torvil, the court wise man. What about him?"

"I have no idea at all, Ronni, but we know the king well enough to know he'll have his reasons, good ones."

Rhonda sighed and stepped back from the bench, rubbing the kinks out of her back. "Yeah. I guess. What would you bet Queen Sally's been having visions again?"

"That could very well be the case. Have you asked him about it yet?"

"No, not yet."

"Why not?"

"I'm afraid of the answer, I suppose. You know me, Clara. I have authority issues; can you see me in command?"

Her friend turned to grin at her. "Yeah, actually, I can. Ronni, don't start panicking here, the king is immortal, too. He's not likely to leave the throne any time soon. I'd say you have a few centuries to get used to the idea."

"I suppose. You know, that's an idea I still can't really wrap my head around."

"What's that?"

"Being immortal. I mean, I know I am, but I still can't really grasp it, you know?"

"I guess. Come on, let's go for coffee. We're just spinning our wheels now."

As they entered the dining hall, seeking the coffee urn that was always ready, they spotted Queen Sally smiling at them. "Oh dear me, I think I've forgotten something in the lab." Clara grinned as she turned and fled.

"Clara Bynes, you get your ass back here." It did no good, as she merely laughed and vanished down the hallway.

"Are you all right, Ronni?"

"No, my queen, I'm not."

"What's wrong?"

"You're going to tell me something I don't want to hear, and my best friend just abandoned me to face it alone."

Sally laughed and took Rhonda by the arm. "Come on, it's not all that bad. Let's get a coffee and I'll tell you about it."

"You've been having visions, something to do with me, right?" asked Rhonda, as she poured her mug full and followed the queen to the table.

"Yes, I have."

"And that's why the king is playing big brother lately."

"Saw through that, did you?"

"Wasn't so hard. Sally, what have you seen?"

"It's a long way off in the future, Ronni, thousands of years, but I keep getting the visions. In those visions, you're the queen of our people. In some of them you're at war with the humans, others show everyone living in harmony, and still others show the non-humans still in hiding."

"Okaay ..."

"There are three things common to all of those visions, Ronni. You're the queen, you have the same three close companions, and you have thousands of werewolves worshiping you."

"Three companions?"

"Gudrun, Ella, and Victor; plus the wolves. They're always there with you."

"Just the four of us? That's all are left?"

"Oh no, girl, I get the sense there are more, plenty more, but I can't see them. Whatever power is guiding this wants me to focus on you."

Rhonda sighed and drained her mug. "So the king is grooming me for his job. I don't want it, Sally, I don't. I don't want to be responsible for all the people. I can barely look after myself, I have authority issues, I'm way too young, I have no experience, I ..."

"And it's clear to me that, at some point in the distant future, you will become the savior of our people. Ronni, Harald knows about these visions. He's trying to prepare you for what will come; and it will come, girl, whether you want it to or not."

Rhonda sighed and let her shoulders sag. "I believe you, my queen. Your visions are rarely wrong, and never three times in a row. This is far in the future, right? There's no rush, is there?" She stopped speaking as she noticed Sally's attention had drifted.

"Crap, something's wrong in the great hall. Come on." She hurried away with Rhonda right behind her. They arrived to find Terry Sawchuk writhing on the floor in pain. "Ronni, get your bag." Rhonda raced away to the lab.

Captured

The vampire hunters sat together in the tavern, talking quietly among themselves. They were here on a training exercise; they planned to capture a dangerous man they'd tracked to this small town in Finland.

They marked him well, and when he rose to follow the slightly drunk woman from the building, the hunters rose silently and followed him, arming themselves with the tranquilizer guns.

The tall blonde woman staggered slightly as she exited the bar. She hadn't gone far when she was grabbed, a hand placed over her mouth, and she was dragged into an alley. The attacker spun her around and tried to slap her across the mouth, but she caught his wrist, and what he saw stopped him cold. She was taller, more muscular, and had a leonine face with long fangs.

He tried to run, but her fangs bit deep into his neck and he was helpless in her grasp. A sudden feeling of unease caused her to turn towards the mouth of the alley, but even as she moved she felt the sting as several tranquilizer darts pierced her skin. She thrust her victim away and turned to fight, but strong nets were thrown over her and she settled to the ground as the drug took effect. Her attempts to use the compulsion failed as the attackers were wearing hearing protection.

Gudrun slowly returned to consciousness, becoming aware of the pain first. Her jaws ached from being forced to remain open by a heavy ball gag, and her arms and legs were bound tightly with razor wire that was biting into her skin.

"Do not move, do not attempt to use that voice of command on me, and do not attempt to transform as your bonds are made of heavy wire. Attempt to transform and you will slice yourself to ribbons. I know what you are, vampire.

"Know that, even as my wife suffered, you will suffer greatly before you die. I am aware of how to make you stay dead, and, in the end, I will toss your severed head into the ocean then burn and bury your body in the mountains. You have slain your last human, demon of hell." The old man laughed and kicked her face before closing the back door of the truck and driving away.

TERRY SAWCHUK LAY MOANING in pain, several people gathered around him. As the captor kicked Gudrun's face, he screamed and grabbed his own face. There was a sudden jab in his arm, then a moment later his consciousness began to fade. "Sorry, Sire, I had to do that. He doesn't know where they've taken her, and I can't let him suffer like this."

"You're right, Ronni. Sedating him was best." The king rose from where he crouched, Terry held easily in his arms. "I'll take him to his room. Tommy, see what you can do to locate her. Igor, assemble a rescue team." With that, he strode away with the unconscious man in his arms.

The young werewolf turned to the people gathered round. "Eric, prepare the plane and your men, Ronni, I'll need you, as well as Gudrun's team." The woman known as Lady Hawk nodded and walked away, her thumbs flying on her phone. Igor turned back to the man at the computer. "Tommy, talk to me."

"Gudrun stayed in Europe while the rest of her people came on ahead. She wanted to check on a few things for Peter, to make sure his facility is secure. She was driving up from Helsinki when she suddenly vanished, and Terry collapsed."

"He said she'd been tranquilized or something, then he started moaning saying she was being tortured. I've got a location for the village where she disappeared, but that's all. Perhaps Queen Sally could give you more."

"Thanks, Tommy, I'll go ask her."

Igor found the queen in her study, holding the chief of the household staff by the hands. Both women were psychic, and together they were stronger. He waited patiently until they opened their eyes. "Were you waiting to learn of Gudrun, Igor?"

"Da. What can you tell me, Queen Sally?"

"She was captured by a madman. He's completely deranged, knows what she is, and he plans to kill her, destroy her utterly. Igor, he knows how to do this. We can't learn anything real about this man, but we do know she's been taken far away from where she was."

"What more can you tell me?"

"There's more than one of them. He's torturing her and enjoying it. This is one sick and twisted individual. She's being held in some sort of dungeon, I think. There's a castle high on a hill, a hill barren of any life. I can't say for certain, but I believe there were guards."

Igor nodded thoughtfully, then turned away. "Thank you, ladies." He returned to the great hall where some of the others were waiting for him.

He sat, lost in thought for a while. "Tommy, can you show me a map of the area where Miss Gudrun disappeared?"

"Coming right up."

A moment later the map appeared on the wall screen. Igor gazed at it for a moment then traced the one main road with his finger. "Show me the topography of this area," he said, as he swept his hand out from her last known location towards the Sanctuary on the Russo-Finnish border lands.

At this point the king returned. "What's this, Igor?"

"Miss Gudrun was driving from Finland to here, Sire. Her last known location was at Imatra, here. I spoke with Queen Sally; she and Elaine had been seeking a location for us. They saw only a castle on a high cliff with nothing growing, only bare stone. They said she is far from where she was taken at Imatra."

"So you're looking for a castle within driving distance of Imatra?"

"Da. Whoever took her wouldn't want to be on the road any longer than necessary. Queen Sally says far from Imatra, so I'm thinking maybe four hours by road, six at most?"

"Makes sense," mused Harald. "What's next?"

"Satellite photos. Mr. Tommy, see if you can find us a possible castle."

"Working. Okay, there's nothing between Imatra and the sanctuary in Russia that fits the bill, so that leaves two options, north or south. South is more heavily populated, so let's try north first."

It took a while, but they found one. Harald called for Sally and she came, looked hard at the image. "I don't believe that's it," she mused, as she studied the image. "I didn't see it from the air, so I can't be certain. It could be it, but I don't think so."

Igor printed off a road map of the area, waiting impatiently for the machine to spit out what he needed. He marked the location of the castle then spoke again. "Keep looking, Mr. Tommy. There must be others."

In the end they marked four possibilities before Sally gasped and pointed at the screen. "That's it, that's what we saw. There's a small village in the nearby forest, but the area around the castle is barren."

"Then this is where we begin."

"This doesn't look good, Igor," mused Tommy. He had a much closer view of the castle now. There were several vehicles in the courtyard, and plenty of figures could be seen moving about.

"Da, many guards, bare ground with no cover. This will not be easy."

Sally gripped his arm tightly. "He plans to kill her, Igor, and he knows how. I have no idea how much time you have, but he's enjoying torturing her, dragging it out. He has a companion, a younger man. They're both torturing her. They're utter madmen, Harald."

The king gently took his wife into his arms. "Easy, my love, easy. Choose your team, Igor."

"Yes, Sire. I will take Lady Hawk and Gudrun's team."

"Is that all?"

"No, Sire. I'll need another vampire, and lots more wolves. I'd like to have Peter and Grandfather's pack as well as Justine, if that's possible."

With a twinkle in her eye, Rhonda gave him the arched eyebrow. "And just what do you want with Justine, my fine furry friend?"

Igor turned and kissed her on the forehead. "Sadly, my beloved, if all else fails, it will fall to you and the mouse to get Miss Gudrun free."

"Igor?"

"Queen Sally, if I can't find another way into that castle, then Ronni will have to fly in with the mouse. It will be up to them to set her free, then she can fight her own way out. We know she can do this.

"I need the wolves to help me take out the guards, and I need Peter to tell me if she's actually in there. A vampire knows when another is near, do they not? Queen Sally, you know I'd never risk my Lady Hawk if I have any other option. The attack of the hawk and mouse is the last resort."

"Actually, I think we should go in first," mused Rhonda, gazing at the satellite picture of the castle, "catch them by surprise. What do you think, Sire?"

"Sadly, I must agree with you. Time is of the essence here, and we have no idea what this madman might do if he thought he was under attack. You need to get in there and set her free before he knows you're coming."

"Then once we find this place, you will take over, my pretty bird. We should go, people."

"Godspeed," said the king. "I'll call ahead and have the others waiting for you at Imatra. Ronni, a word in private before you go."

"Oh course, Sire."

Both Igor and Rhonda gave the king a questioning look, but he was already on the way to his study. Rhonda followed closely while Igor went to pack what they would need. Harald went to his chair by the window and indicated Rhonda should join him.

She sat gracefully, facing him then spoke. "Harald, what is it? You've been big brothering me for weeks now. What's going on? Are you plotting against me?"

"Ronni, I need you to get this thing under control and quickly, but I also need you to be extra careful."

"Me? Talk to me, Sire. What's going on in that head of yours?"

The king sighed and relaxed back in his chair for a moment then leaned forward again. "When you went with Igor to bring back the were-horse, there was a moment of tension between you."

Rhonda bristled a bit at that. "I don't see how ..."

"Ronni, that was a tense time for us all. When Sally realized you two might be having problems, she tried to look ahead in time to see what a break up between you could mean for us all."

"Okay, but it wasn't like that, and we sorted it out between us like any couple would do. I don't get the connection."

"The danger was exposure to the general public, Ronni. You know what that could mean."

"All right, so what did the queen see?"

"She tried to see the immediate future, but what she saw was thousands of years beyond that. She saw you as queen, with Gudrun and Victor at your side and Ella at your feet. Before you were thousands of werewolves. They all knelt to you and the alpha warned you the human army was approaching. You declared it was time to meet them head on.

"Sally said you were hard as stone, and the vampires obeyed you instantly."

"Yes, she told me, but that future was broken when Igor and I reconciled, wasn't it?"

"It was, but she's since seen more, without the war against the humans, but in each you rule with Gudrun at your side. Sally believes these visions are thousands of years in the future, but one thing seems clear to me."

"And that is?"

"You're a natural leader, and our people will need you."

"And that's why you've been acting like my big brother, you've been trying to mentor me."

Again, the king sighed deeply. "Yes. Ronni ..."

"I get it, Sire. I know I'm a bit of a wild child, but I get it. Listen, I need you to know that I'm utterly devoted to you and to our people. I was lost, injured, terrified, and you folks took me in, gave me a new and better life, and a man to love who has no equal.

"Look, those futures are a long way off, and anything can happen to change them completely, but I get it. I trust the queen's visions. I need to learn how to lead wisely, and so much more. You can start teaching me as soon as we get back."

"Just promise me you'll be careful, come back in one piece."

"I swear it, I'll be careful."

"All right then, you'd better hurry, Igor will be pacing by now." With a laugh she ran from his study.

The king gazed out the window and sighed. "One day you will succeed me, Lady Hawk. For the sake of our people, I hope you'll be ready."

Pain

"It hurts, doesn't it?" asked the man, as he squatted down near Gudrun's battered body. It was a different man than before, a younger man. "I know it hurts because I have studied how to tie up a person in such a way, and I've practiced many times. In a few days it will be the fortieth anniversary of the day that scar-faced abomination destroyed my mother.

"Oh, he didn't kill her, not at first. First he tortured her, then he let another that looked like you feed on her, torment her until she swooned, and then he waited until she revived before killing her. He then killed the second vampire and walked away, leaving me to die slowly in that burning church. I was helped by another of his victims who managed to survive as well. He raised me as his own and, together, we have plotted our revenge.

"From that day to this, we have hunted for your kind. We've managed to find three over the years and make such an end of them as this, but scar-face has eluded us. No matter, we have trained others. Even after we're dead and gone, the hunt will go on."

He grabbed her by the hair and jerked her head back so he could look into her eyes. "Do you hear me, demon of hell? The hunt will go on until none are left, your kind eradicated from the face of the earth." With a muttered curse in Russian, he thrust her head away and rose to walk from the room, leaving her there on the cold stone floor.

Gudrun could hear him talking to another outside the room. They were gloating, one suggested they might make sport of her body before the killing, but he said no. "The cursed thing is unclean, unfit for a man to touch. No, we will torment it as it has tormented others then, on the anniversary of my mother's death, we will drag it out here, spread it across that stone, and dismember it, then I will cut off the head and carry it away to the sea."

He walked away then, leaving the two guards behind at her door. "I'm not so sure about all this," said one. "He's been preaching this for years, but all I see is a woman being tortured. It could be his sister-in-law for all we know."

"What do we care, we sing the song like true believers, and he pays us well."

"I wouldn't care if he'd just kill her, it's the torture I don't like, waste of a good woman."

"So you'd rather torture her with a friendly weapon?"

"Da, I would indeed. Poor soul won't live long enough to reach his magic anniversary though, the way he abuses her."

Gudrun turned her attention away from them. She fought the pain, the weakness, and took in some of her surroundings, as much as possible from her position on the cold floor. Deep breaths helped to focus her mind, clear her vision. There, above the door, a camera aimed right at her, the bastards were watching her, enjoying her torment.

She silently vowed revenge. These men had obviously survived one of Mobutu's mad killing frenzies, probably brought on by his inability to track down Peter. This mess would be a nightmare to clean up.

Carefully, she inspected her prison with her eyes, moving as little as possible. Somehow she would escape the razor wire bonds that held her, she would leave this place and a trail of dead bodies behind. It wasn't in her nature to give up. Gudrun ignored the pain and fed her rage instead, waiting for darkness.

As the light left the sky, she bit down hard on the huge ball gag in her mouth. It didn't give at all, but she felt the strap that held it flex ever so slightly. If she could only work it loose enough to be able to speak. She could then use the compulsion to command her captors to set her free.

WHILE GUDRUN STRUGGLED to stay conscious and find a way to free herself, Rhonda ran to the hangar where Igor and the mercenaries were waiting. She hopped on board and Igor shut and sealed the door. "Go, Eric."

"Where?"

"Imatra, Finland. Peter should send you coordinates long before we get there."

"Strap in." The plane rose swiftly then shot away, well below the radar. It wasn't until they were out over the Atlantic Ocean that the plane rose to high altitude.

Igor sat gazing at Rhonda as the plane took off. "What?"

"You tell me, sweet Ronni. The king spoke to you in private. Should I ask about this?"

She snuggled closer to him and spoke. "I was right, sweetheart. Harald has been playing big brother, mentoring me. Queen Sally's been star-gazing into a distant future. She's had different visions, but with one central theme.

"She sees me as the queen with Gudrun at my side and thousands of wolves kneeling, fist raised in the air, hailing me as queen. Harald didn't say it, but Sally said he sees me as his heir now and is trying to teach me how to be a good leader."

"How far in the future?"

"Thousands of years at best guess. It'll take a lot of generations to produce that many wolves."

"So, my pretty bird, how do you feel about this?"

"Truth? I'm scared shitless, Igor. I never wanted anything like this, I don't want this now."

"But?"

"If it's going to come, I need to be ready. If I'm going to end up as the one who has to protect our people, then I need to learn all I can about leadership, about everything."

"Da." Igor nodded his head slowly then sighed. "All right, my pretty bird, you're in charge, this is your case now."

"What? Igor, no. Jesus, what the hell are you thinking?"

"I'm thinking I won't live forever; I'm thinking the one you'll need to help you in the future is being held prisoner, tortured. You need to get her free, let her see that it's you she can depend on to have her back. Take command, queen of the werewolves, get this done."

Wide-eyed, Rhonda stared at him, he was serious. Her mighty alpha was actually going to make her take command, and she didn't want anything to do with it. The Lady Hawk was scared to death.

What if she failed and lost Gudrun? What if she got everybody killed in the process? What if she screwed up and the whole thing, the existence of the non-humans, became fully exposed to the world. She swallowed hard and slowly spoke a single word. "Okay."

Igor hugged her close. "It's all right, my pretty bird, you always tell me what to do anyway, this just makes it official."

She poked him in the ribs. "Shut up, you beast. Igor."

"Yeah?"

"Don't let me mess this up."

"You won't, my love. You must become the queen of the werewolves, and so now you are. I'm the pack alpha, but you're the queen of us all."

"Igor?"

"It's what I wanted all along anyway, sweet Ronni. I've been trying to devise a way to ensure that, once I'm gone, the wolves will look to you for guidance, leadership."

"Igor?"

"We can't have pups, my love, so this is how my line will go on, how my pack will remain under my guidance. Now, tell me everything you know about Queen Sally's visions."

Rhonda did as he asked, and then she snuggled deeper into his embrace, nodding her head. She'd do this for him, for Gudrun, for the king, and for all the people who'd taken her in and given her a life worth living. If this was to be her fate, she might as well embrace it. At no point did she doubt Sally's visions, they'd proven accurate far too often for that.

The plane sped over the churning waters far below, the king called and briefed Peter, who then briefed his people, and the Lady Hawk tried to think her way through the coming rescue mission. The coast of Britain was coming in sight as Igor's phone rang.

"Igor."

"Igor, it's Peter," said that deep voice. "Harald has briefed us on the emergency. We are yours to command, what do you need?"

"I'm not leading this mission, Peter. The Lady Hawk is. I'll put her on." He passed her the phone.

With a sigh, she took it from his hand. "Peter?"

"Rhonda, this is your mission?"

"It is."

"What do you need?"

"I need a vampire to confirm she is actually in the place we suspect. The land surrounding the castle is bare of vegetation, I'll need a few wolves to scout around, see if they can find us a hidden way into the castle. I'll also need Justine. She and I will make the first incursion, try to find Gudrun, and set her free before her captors realize there's a rescue attempt."

"And once she's free?"

"We'll make an end of those who took her, but also find out what they know, how they knew, how many more are aware of us, then we'll have to clean this mess up, but first we get Gudrun free."

"Agreed. We're leaving right now, what else do you need? Should I bring blood for her?"

"No need. I'm going to feed those bastards to her one at a time. Can you meet us on the highway outside Imatra?"

"On our way, Lady Hawk."

He broke the connection and she passed the phone back to Igor. She returned to her brooding with a deep sigh. Finally she stood and made her way forward to the cockpit. "Better slow us down a bit, Eric. Peter just left home. It'll take him a while to reach a likely spot."

He nodded and adjusted the speed. "Swinging north, around Norway and Sweden, we'll come down from there to the pick-up point. Do we have a pick-up point yet?"

"Not yet. I'll let you know the instant we do." He nodded that he understood, she returned to her seat beside Igor and snuggled into his arms. She felt safe there, protected. Rhonda took what comfort she could from her lover's arms while there was time, and that time was running short.

AT THE RUSSIAN COMPOUND, Peter was issuing orders, gathering his people. "Illya, we have an emergency. Gudrun's been taken, Igor is on the way to get her back. He wants some wolves and a vampire to assist. You and I will go, bring four more wolves, fighters, and bring Justine."

"Me?" asked Justine, coming out of her lab with Nikka close behind. She'd learned enough Russian to follow a basic conversation.

Peter turned to her, effortlessly shifting into English. "Yes, she asked specifically for you. She said you and she would make the first incursion."

"She?"

"Yes, Rhonda. Igor told me she's leading this mission. I expect she'll enlighten us when they arrive. We have to hurry now."

"Where are we going?"

"Finland."

Justine had no further chance for questions. Nikka passed her a long thick fur coat and she swept it around her shoulders then hurried after her young friend. Outside there was instant rebellion. Illya forbid Nikka to go, but she insisted.

"Grandfather, I'm a woman grown now, Igor is coming, Ronni is leading the mission, you have to let me help, let me take my full place in the pack."

He looked like he would object further, but Justine interfered. "Illya, there's no time for this. I'll keep her out of trouble. Let's go."

"Bring extra vehicles," shouted Peter, as he and Illya climbed into one car, "We'll be picking up passengers."

They went in five cars, Peter leading the way. They pushed the speed as hard as they dared, and soon reached the border crossing. This sudden appearance of several vehicles at once caused instant suspicion. As Peter got out of the car, several guns were swiftly pointed in his direction, but the voice of compulsion soon had everything under control.

Justine and Nikka had a car to themselves. Neither said anything until they were well past the border and into Finland. Finally, Nikka spoke softly. "Justine, do you know fully what's going on?"

"No, my sister, I don't, but it seems a lot has happened since we left the Lair. It appears that Rhonda is in command now, not Igor, and I wonder what's going on with that. I do remember her as being a take charge woman, though. It used to piss off a lot of the older guys.

"Anyway, something's happened to Gudrun. I believe she's been taken captive, and Rhonda wants me to join her as the rescue team."

"Why you? I mean, why not Igor, or one of the vampires? Why my sister, the mouse?"

"I have no idea, but I suspect it must be a hard place to get into. A hawk and a mouse can go many places a wolf or vampire could never reach."

"Da, that's true."

"So, why the big fuss to go along? I know you want to see Igor, but still ...?"

"I thought it would be exciting, but now Igor's not the alpha anymore and Rhonda is leading. Now I'm just worried."

"I understand, honey. Look, we'll soon be there and then we'll know what's going on."

Paving the Way to the Future

Hours later the king was still in his study, gazing out the window, lost in thought. A voice at the door brought his attention back. "You wanted to see me, Sire?"

Harald chuckled as he turned back to the room. "Yes, Larise. Could you see if you can find Ella for me?"

"Elaine's already on it, they'll be here in a minute."

"Well you don't have to look so smug. You psychic women sure do make my life easier though. Larise, give me your opinion of the Lady Hawk."

"Rhonda? I like the woman, Sire. If anybody at all has a right to hate me or resent me, it would be Rhonda, but she doesn't. I love her for that forgiveness, and I'll admit I go the extra mile for her every chance I get.

"Let's see, she's the alpha female of the wolf pack, no mistaking that. Bran says Igor's made it plain that, if anything should happen to him, the pack must look to Rhonda for leadership, and Bran swears he will. I know my wolf well, Sire, and he means it. She kept him alive, helped and supported him when it all went wrong out west. He worships the woman.

"So, are you going to make Ronni your heir to the throne?"

"All right, young woman, how did you come to that conclusion? The mark doesn't give you that much insight into my thought processes. Now talk."

Larise grinned at him as he tried and failed to give her a stern look. "Sire, you've been playing big brother to Rhonda for weeks now, and Elaine was talking about opening up the guest rooms, getting them ready for company, laying in extra supplies for the kitchen and cleaning staff.

"That tells me something big is on the go, you're planning to call everybody here for something, probably to do with Rhonda since you asked about her, so I wondered if, since you've been mentoring her and all, you were planning to make the announcement, make her the official heir."

The king chuckled and shook his head. "You're good, Larise. Yes, you read it right. That's my plan, but it all depends on Ella."

"She's the strongest, loved and respected by all, yes, you will need her support for sure."

"What about you, Larise? How do you feel about this?"

"I like it, Sire, but it really doesn't matter."

"Of course it does, I value your opinion."

"No, Sire, what I mean is, she only comes to the throne if you die, and if you die, I cease to exist. Rhonda can't mark anyone to ensure their loyalty, their silence, return them to themselves. However, if you simply abdicated, and told me to choose my path, I'd work for her, no problem."

He nodded thoughtfully. "Thank you, Larise. You can relax, I'm not going anywhere. This is just in case the worst happens. All monarchies have to have an heir to the throne."

"With a visible heir, it prevents a lot of in-fighting for the succession if the ruling monarch suddenly dies?"

"Precisely."

"So, are we keeping this secret?"

"Only until I gain Ella's approval."

"Ella's approval for what, Harald?" came her voice from the doorway.

"That's my cue to scoot." Larise grinned as she leaped to her feet, smiled at Ella, then hurried out of the room.

"You wanted to see me, Harald?"

"Yes, Mother, on a matter of some importance."

"Is it about securing Gudrun's return?"

"No, I have every confidence Rhonda will secure her release."

"Rhonda? Not Igor? Harald, what's going on?"

"Ella, recently Sally's had a number of visions of a distant future. In one we were at war with the humans, in another we lived openly in harmony with them, and in yet another we were in hiding as we are now.

"Each of these visions had three things in common. The Lady Hawk was queen of the non-humans, there were thousands of werewolves hailing her as their monarch, utterly devoted to her, and in each she had the same close companions as guards and advisors, Gudrun, Victor, and you."

"And the other vampires? The horse, Torvil? What about the rest?"

"Ella, I didn't see the others, nor did I look for everybody," said the queen, as she entered the room. "I was actually trying to see a more immediate future, but somehow I keep getting thrown far out in time, too far to put any real faith in what I've seen, but the common thread bears attention."

"Rhonda."

"Yes, Mother," sighed the king. "Please give us your impressions of our Lady Hawk."

Ella West nodded thoughtfully. "All right, Harald. For me, she's a bit wild and impulsive, but that's the hawk influence in her, I guess. She's terribly young, but I suspect she'll have a few centuries to gain experience.

"While working with Rhonda and Igor out west I saw them in action and liked what I saw. Yes, Ronni's impulsive, but devoted to Igor, to all of us, and she worked hard, extremely hard, often taking charge. She risked her life to save Kylie, and for that she has my undying gratitude.

"If you think she's the right one, and you're planning to mentor her, Harald, I'll support your decision, and your choice." The king sighed and sat back.

"You were concerned?"

"Yes, Ella, I was. You're the strongest of us all, and the most beloved, respected. Truth is, most will see you as the natural choice, or Gudrun if you declined. Rhonda is the wild card all right."

"I do understand. Harald, I believe you're probably right about this, especially in light of Sally's visions. Mobutu pointed out to me clearly that I shouldn't be the queen, I don't have the knack for it, nor do I want it. Go ahead, I'll support you and the Lady Hawk fully."

"Thank you, Mother. I believe that, with yours and Gudrun's support, everyone will accept this."

"First she has to get Gudrun back for us."

"She will, Ella," said the queen. "This is the turning point, the place where Rhonda learns she was born to lead, and where she gains Gudrun's complete support. It'll be tense, difficult, but I have full confidence in her ability to succeed here."

"You weren't so sure of her a few weeks ago."

"No, and my doubts at that time led to these visions. Rhonda proved herself worthy of our trust, our faith in her on that mission. She knows when to lead and to follow, she has keen insights into what needs to happen and acts quickly."

"Yes, and now I need to teach her to take a few more people into her confidence before flying off to save the world," grumbled the king.

Ella rose and, smiling as she patted his shoulder, headed for the door. "I leave you to it, my king. Congratulations, you're a father." She was still chuckling as she walked away.

"Well that's a relief," said the king. "Now we wait and see how this goes in Finland."

At that point his phone rang. "Yes?"

"Harald, it's Peter. Are you aware Igor has abdicated his position as lead agent in favor of the Lady Hawk?"

"Igor has only done what I desired, Peter. Between us, she is to be appointed the heir. Ella has already expressed her support for this decision."

"Then you may add mine as well. I trust you, Harald, and I trust your judgment. I will serve the Lady Hawk as though it were you giving the direction."

"Thank you, Peter. Keep an eye on her, do what you can to help her."

"As you desire, my king." The connection broke and Harald dropped the phone on his desk. "Well, Peter's vote is in. I think we're in the clear on this, my love."

"Now we have to hope she'll be willing to accept it."

"Yes, well, there is that."

"And then there's the other."

"Sally? The other?"

"Igor."

"Beloved, I'm not keeping up here, what about Igor?"

"In the visions Rhonda is queen over all, my lover, especially the werewolves. That is unlikely to happen unless ..."

"Unless Igor suddenly takes over. Well, bugger. I'll bet that's why he left the rest of his pack here. He's planning to challenge Illya."

"Harald, do you think he would?"

"Igor's a lot smarter than he lets on. I'll bet he's figured it out and plans to bring them all under his lead."

"There's more to it than that, Sire." Branimir was standing in the doorway. "Forgive the intrusion, but Elaine said you'd be looking for me."

"Blast that girl," chuckled Harald. "She knows what I'm thinking before I do. Come in, Bran. Tell me what I'm missing here. What more is there?"

"Sire, Igor is well aware there will be no pups from his beloved Lady Hawk. There is only one way for him to leave this world knowing his people are led by the strongest alpha. Our pack, the Clan of the Hawk, is utterly devoted to Miss Ronni. I'm the next strongest, and Igor has sworn me to obey the Lady Hawk should anything ever happen to him. That, I will do gladly.

"Igor told me before they left that he plans to bring the Children of the Wolf under his, and eventually Lady Hawk's, rule; sworn to the vampire king's service. With Ronni in command of the wolves down through the generations, Igor's rule and guidance will continue. He will have no pups to pass his trust to, so he will pass it to her. All werewolves will obey her, and she will keep them safe.

"So, what did you want to see me about, Sire?"

"Just this, Bran. Are the wolves truly so devoted to Rhonda?"

"Da, that and more," he grinned.

A Bad Feeling

Gudrun's consciousness faded in and out, hiding her from the pain in her tortured body. The younger man had become infuriated when he realized his silver cross had no effect on her at all, so he beat her savagely with it. He'd also noticed her body was trying to heal itself, so he began to torment her more often, to keep her weakened.

Alone in his makeshift office, a cold stone cell once occupied by monks centuries past, Johan sat staring at the wooden stake. The cross had no effect on her, would the stake? What else was wrong about the legends? Could they actually manage to kill her, or would she magically come back? Had he sealed his own doom and that of the chosen people they'd managed to convert to the cause?

He turned the wood in his hand, feeling the texture, taking comfort from the familiar. He'd made it from the shovel handle the vampire had driven through his mother before it ripped out her throat. It was a cold comfort now as doubts and fears assaulted him in the semi-darkness.

The computer screen flickered behind him, making eerie ghostly shadows on the wall, further disturbing his mind. He saw his mother's form in those dancing figures, and his hands tightened on the wooden stake. A part of him wanted to drive it through Melosh's heart.

"The day draws nearer, Mother, when I can rejoin you. We've become the monsters, but we have found them. When the time comes, I'll make an end of Melosh for what he has made me become, and then I'll join you in the next world. Now it's time to learn more of the vampire."

He surged to his feet and grabbed up a container of water, carefully prying the stopper out of the glass mouth. Holy water. He'd been saving it for the final day, but now he had to know. A cup of the precious liquid in his hand, he returned the stopper then strode out and down the corridor to her cell.

She was still lying where he'd left her, or was she? Had he left her facing the other way? A hand grabbed her hair and jerked her around to face the door. "You stay where I put you or you will be punished. I will now enjoy your screams as your face burns away." With that he hurled the holy water into her face.

The water was like ambrosia as some of it trickled into her dry and tortured mouth, and she moaned, trying to get more of it on her tongue. She grunted as his boot connected with her ribs. Still cursing, he hurled the now empty tin mug against the stone wall and stalked out, leaving her there desperately trying to suck more of the sweet moisture into her mouth.

"Nothing," he snarled, as he smashed the larger container of holy water against the wall of his office. "She actually enjoyed it. More wrong information. So, what information do we have that we know is good? They are susceptible to tranquilizers, they are incredibly strong but can be overcome, silver and the cross are useless, holy water is useless, direct sunlight is next on the list. Tomorrow I haul that accursed abomination out into direct sunlight."

"Relax, Johan, relax, this is a learning experience," said Melosh, as he entered and sat down. "We told her we had done this before, but it was a lie. She's the first and we found her by accident, but we did find her. Accident, no, I believe it's god's will. It's up to us to expose the truth of their existence. Once we convince our own people, we will show the videos to the proper authorities, bring witnesses, and then the hunt begins, yes?"

"Perhaps, but so much of what we believe is wrong. The only thing that was true so far is her ability to heal herself. Silver has no effect, the cross has no effect, holy water she enjoyed, ..."

"And so we have learned many things that don't work. We have time yet to experiment, to learn more before the anniversary arrives.

One thing I'm certain of, cut off the head and whatever it is, human or animal, it dies."

Gudrun's younger tormentor sighed and relaxed back into the chair. "Da, I remember the scar-faced one did that to kill the others. At least there is that. We know that fire burns her like it does us, but nothing more, holy water, silver, and the cross are useless. The stake is unknown, sunlight unknown, she bleeds if cut, and she breathes, has a heartbeat, so, not living dead.

"She is warm to the touch, so, not cold reanimated corpse. What they are in reality, we don't know, but this we do know for certain, they're pure evil and must be destroyed." He drifted off into his own thoughts and the older man left him to it.

Back in Gudrun's cell, a rat cautiously approached and sniffed at her. She looked into its eyes and saw only the hunger there, the desire for a meal. Slowly, carefully, she raised her head as far as her bonds would allow. It hurt like hellfire, but she got some height with her chin. The rat moved in closer, sniffing at her face.

Fighting the pain, Gudrun pulled her head back further causing the rat to take another step forward. Cautiously, the animal took that last fateful step to its doom. Her head crashed down on its body, crushing the life from it. The sharp wire that dug into her neck also cut into the body of the rat, making it bleed.

She sucked in her breath hard and managed to get a few drops of precious blood into her mouth around the gag. It wasn't much, just a tease, but it fed her thirst, calling to the beast within her. She let the killing lust rise up to hide the pain and allow the few drops of blood feed her depleted healing abilities.

In the morning he would find the dead rat and punish her, but for now, by pressing the body with her face, she was able to squeeze out a few more drops of the life giving blood. Now it was dark, for now there was a faint hope, and she nursed it, working away at her bonds, trying to ignore the pain.

"What's wrong with you?" one guard asked the other, as they slowly paced back and forth outside Gudrun's cell.

"I just had a bad feeling, like something walked across my grave."

"Perhaps the vampire got loose and is hunting," chuckled his companion.

"It's not funny, something is out there, it's coming for her. We're all going to die."

"Pah, you gypsies are all alike."

"Romany. I've told you many times, the word is Romany."

"Yeah, yeah, you're still spooky."

In his office, the brooding man looked up as his elderly mentor entered again. "Johan, I fear something might be amiss. I've had a bad feeling."

"Da, me too, a cold hand running up my spine. Tell the guards to keep a sharp eye out. That vampire's not going anywhere, but there may be another looking for her. Perhaps she has a mate who seeks for us."

"That does make sense. We should prepare to receive unwelcome visitors." Melosh turned and walked out. A moment later the entire compound and surrounding area was suddenly bathed in strong lights.

RHONDA LEANED ACROSS Eric's shoulder. "Peter's almost there. He's a few miles from the castle at an open spot where we could hide the plane. Here's the coordinates."

"Got it. Touchdown in five, we're nearly there."

She returned to her seat and cuddled back into Igor's arms. "We've only got a few more minutes before we land, my love. Are you going to tell me what's going through your mind?"

Igor tightened his arms around her and sighed. "I trust Queen Sally's visions, my pretty bird. Once we land, you will have to get Miss Gudrun back for us, I have another task."

"Igor?"

"The wolves, my love. Our pack worships you, but Grandfather's pack does not know you well. My task is to bring them into our control."

"Igor?"

"I will not kill my grandfather, sweet Ronni, but before we leave for home you will be the queen of the wolves. All will acknowledge you, I must see to this, and I will. We'll be there to help you, but I will challenge for dominance and defeat Grandfather."

"Sweetheart, please don't do that. If I can't win them over myself, then there's no way for me to hold them anyway. There's no need to confront Illya." He just nodded and kissed the top of her head as the plane shuddered slightly then began to settle to the ground.

THE FIVE CARS WERE pulled off the lonely road, their occupants waiting, each lost in their own thoughts. "What is it Illya?"

"I suddenly had a premonition of my own death."

"Oh?"

"In the jaws of a wolf. Ah, just an old man's fears, Peter, pay no heed to it. Just a bad feeling, nothing more." His companion nodded, the plane was landing.

Arrival

The plane touched down and the passengers leaped out. Gudrun's mercenaries swiftly pulled the tarp out of the cargo hold and draped it over the aircraft. Peter stepped out of the car and approached. "We're here and ready, Rhonda. What's our next move?"

"Are we between Imatra and the castle?"

"Yes, it and the village beyond are several miles away."

"Do you have transport for us?"

"Yes, there, that one, Victor is driving. How do you want to approach this?"

"I want to get close, but well back out of sight. I ..."

She was interrupted by two voices shouting at once. "Igor!" Igor looked up to catch Justine in his arms. She hugged him tightly, then kissed him. "Hey you, stop kissing my husband."

"Oh stop being such a jealous bitch, Ronni," grinned Justine, as she released Igor and stepped toward Rhonda, "I'll kiss you too."

"You do, and I'll pinch your ass in public," laughed Rhonda, as she hugged Justine tightly. "Damn, you look good. Enjoying life over here?"

"I am, Ronni. Look at this, can you imagine wearing this fur coat back in America?"

"Oh hell no, the animal rights people would shoot you on sight."

"I know, right? So, you're in charge?"

"Yup. Not my idea, but what can you do?"

"Yeah. I take it this is a tough place to get into?"

"It is. I'm hoping I can land you someplace where you can sneak inside, then unlock the door and let me in. The plan is to cut Gudrun loose and let her eat the lot of those bastards."

"Good idea. How the hell did they manage to capture her anyway?"

"I have no idea, but I intend to find out and make damn sure it never happens again."

They turned to see Nikka hugging Igor and Illya standing slightly aside. Igor released Nikka then spoke to Peter. "That big car is for us, yeah? Cool. Come. Let's get on the go. Grandfather, you and the wolves ride together at the back of the line."

Illya's eyes went hard and Rhonda sighed. "Ah, crap."

Justine looked puzzled. "Ronni, what just happened?"

"Igor just challenged for dominance. I told him it wasn't necessary. Dammit, Igor, this isn't the time for this."

It was far too late at that point. "Did you hear me, Grandfather? I said to move the wolves back."

"Is that a challenge, Igor?"

Suddenly Igor hit the old man on the chest with the flats of his hands, thrusting him back. "Da, I challenge you. I am Igor, alpha of all werewolves. Submit or fight me."

With lightning speed the old man morphed into the wolf and leaped at Igor, but to everyone's surprise, Igor didn't change. He grabbed the old wolf in mid-leap, swung him high, then slammed him hard on the ground. "Submit."

The wolf struggled to get air back in his lungs, but managed it. Again he leapt to his feet and charged. Igor grabbed him and threw him into a swampy puddle, but the wolf jumped up and charged back in. "So be it," growled Igor, as he shimmered into the huge wolf and leaped to meet the oncoming charge.

They met in mid-air then, in a flurry of fangs; they landed with the old wolf on his back with the young giant snarling above him. With a sigh, the Illya wolf relaxed and averted his eyes, full submission.

Igor turned to the others, all the wolves had transformed. As one they dropped to their bellies and looked away in submission. There would be no further challenges. He morphed back into the man and extended his hand to help Illya back to his feet. "Why, Grandfather? Why did you make me hurt you?"

"I am Illya, wolf, a child of the forest. I do not submit to humans."

"So you waited for me to change? Are you crazy?"

Illya grinned at that. "I've been accused of that a few times."

Igor hugged his grandfather tightly. "You old fool, I could have broken your neck."

"You nearly did. So, back of the line?"

Igor sighed deeply. "Doesn't matter, that was just to make the challenge. Peter, you ride with the Lady Hawk, I will ride with Grandfather. We have much to discuss."

"Let's go, people," said Rhonda, as she started toward the cars, "we're wasting time." She shook a warning finger at Igor. "We need to talk."

"It was necessary, sweet Ronni, you know this. Nikka, with us."

They got in the cars and started out. Igor was driving, following the car with Rhonda in it. "You told Rhonda it was necessary, what did you mean by that?" asked Nikka.

"You must forgive me, Grandfather," sighed Igor. "Nikka, Queen Sally has had many visions of a distant future, all are different, but some parts are always the same. Grandfather's wish will come true."

"Igor? What do you mean?" asked Illya.

"In queen Sally's visions, the Lady Hawk is always the queen of all non-human folk, and always there are werewolves, thousands of them. They all transform and kneel, eyes down and a fist raised high in the air. 'Hail to the Queen,' they shout. 'Hail Lady Hawk, Queen of the Wolves.' This is what I've been told.

"That time is far away, but I believe it will come, and with the Lady Hawk to guide them, our people will prosper. This is why I've done this; this is why I challenged you, Grandfather."

"You want to bring this vision into reality. I can understand that."

"Thousands of them, Grandfather. Not two or three packs, but hundreds of packs, united under one main alpha, serving the queen who protects them."

"Ah, she cannot give you pups to pass your leadership to, so you pass it to her, in this way you are alpha forever. It makes sense, Igor. Can you truly trust her with this?"

"I can, I do, and I will to my dying day. First chance you get, talk to Branimir, he can tell you of his experience of the Lady Hawk's devotion to the wolves."

"So why now, Igor?" asked Nikka. "Why not wait for a better moment, why challenge now?"

"Because now is a desperate time. I have put Ronni in charge when she didn't think she was ready. Forgive me, Grandfather, but you are so hard-headed, and you don't like taking orders from the young. This is sweet Ronni's trial by fire, she will need instant obedience."

Illya sighed and squeezed Igor's arm. "I see now what you did and why. It was the right thing to do, Igor. Even if I think her commands are dangerous or stupid, I will obey instantly."

Igor chuckled. "I think this is what Mr. Torvil would call belligerent submission." Illya laughed and squeezed his arm again.

VICTOR WAS DRIVING with Rhonda in the seat beside him, Peter beside the other door. The mercenaries were in the back seat, their gear piled behind them. "Are we there yet?"

"No, Lady Hawk, not yet," chuckled Victor. "It's not far, though, I believe. From the map we bought at Imatra, the road should soon fork, the village to the right, and the road past to the left. We take the road past the village then shortly after that a dirt road turns off to the old castle."

"Do we know anything about this place?"

"Not much," replied Peter. "It was abandoned for decades, then about thirty years ago someone acquired it, but he's been extremely secretive about what he does there. This is all we could learn in Imatra. Perhaps we could learn more in the village."

Rhonda thought for a moment then turned slightly. "Eric, recommendations?"

"There's no time, Lady Hawk. We need to see this place for ourselves."

"Agreed. Let's ... What the hell is that light in the distance?"

"That should be our target," said Victor. "There's the turn to the village, we go this way. I bet that light is the place we seek."

"Yeah, me too. Paranoid bastard, isn't he? Damnation, this won't be easy."

"This looks like our road, Lady Hawk."

"Kill the lights, get all the cars off the main road and out of sight."

Victor shut off the headlights then turned off onto the dirt road, the other cars did the same. They got out of the cars and approached Rhonda who stood gazing up at the light on the hill in the distance. "Are we ready, people?"

"All are ready, sweet Ronni," said Igor.

"All right then, let's go. No flashlights, we don't want them to see us coming." She took barely three steps before she stepped in a puddle of water. "Uh. Shit." With a piercing cry the hawk climbed into the darkened sky as her clothes settled to the ground. Chuckling to himself, Igor gathered them up into a bundle then hurried after the others.

Blood

Gudrun suddenly stiffened, barely breathing, ignoring the pain in her body. She had felt a small shift, something triggering her battered senses. There. It came again, a bit stronger. Another vampire was in the area. Hope flared in her breast as she focused on that sense, that instinct, calling on all her life force. Yes, it was slowly drawing nearer.

The feeling was clearer now, a vampire was drawing closer. No, there were two. She exulted, they had found her. Two vampires traveling together could only mean King Harald's people. Yes, it was clear now, they were slowly getting closer, and she knew them. Peter and Victor. They'd found her, they were coming.

Relief, hope, and fear coursed through her simultaneously. Of course, Sally must have had a vision and Harald sent help. They were aware she'd been taken and were prepared. She would soon be out of the cursed wire that bound her. All she had to do was stay alive. Her one fear now was of that madman cutting off her head before they could set her free.

Movement nearby caught her attention and she nearly panicked. No, not when help was so close. Rolling her eyes as hard as possible, she caught the movement again. Risking everything, she braced herself for the pain the movement would cause, but she did it.

It wasn't much of a move, but it gave her a better view of the door and the small window on the other wall. She was just in time to see a hawk land on the stone windowsill and peck at the heavy wire mesh that covered the window. Rhonda.

The hope swelled in her breast anew. If the Lady Hawk was here, Igor and his wolves wouldn't be far away. If only they could get to her in time. She made eye contact with the bird then turned her gaze to the camera above the door. It took a few tries, but Rhonda got it. The hawk turned her head, looked at the camera, then back to Gudrun and bobbed her head up and down to show she understood, then flew away.

A few moments later her captor came into the cell, grabbed her by the hair and yanked her back around to where he'd had her before. "I've told you before not to move, but you don't listen well. Now I teach you, now I punish you for disobedience."

He tightened the wires that held her, and she screamed around the huge gag in her mouth. A few hard slaps to her face drove the gag deeper, bringing more whimpers of pain from her dry throat. His arm was drawn back to deliver another blow when he noticed her eyes. He released his grip on her, shuddered as he backed off, and then stalked away, back to his cell.

His older companion watched him, puzzled as he poured himself a generous glass of vodka. "It was her eyes, Melosh," he said, in reply to the unspoken question. "Even though I cause her great pain, and she cries out, she is no longer afraid." He shuddered, then tossed down the vodka.

"What do you want to do?"

"Go tell the others, prepare for someone to attempt a rescue, probably the vampire's mate. Arm everyone with tranquilizer weapons. Silver bullets are useless."

The older man hurried away to do his bidding. With a deep sigh and a shiver of fear, Johan scooped up his journal then triggered the secret doorway. Abandoning his one friend to the vampire, he vanished into the darkness of the hidden tunnel. Johan had no doubt Melosh would perish within the hour, at least he hoped he would. He was gone before Rhonda and her troops arrived at the base of the cliff that supported the castle.

THE LADY HAWK RETURNED to her people just as they reached the edge of the forest. Igor helped her into her clothes. "So, did you scout out the target, my pretty bird?"

"Yes, I found her. She's in a cell about halfway up the back wall. The cell has a small window, but it's covered with wire mesh and there's a video camera mounted above the door.

"People, she's in bad shape. They've got her bound with razor wire, so any movement would be torment as well as damaging, and there's a gag of some kind in her mouth so she can't speak. Whoever these people are, they know what they're dealing with. We need to do this right. Igor, we need another way into that castle."

"Da. If it's there, we'll find it. Wolves, we seek another entrance to the castle, a hidden path the warriors can use to surprise the enemy. Spread out and search the area, but don't let them see you." With that, he transformed and raced away through the trees. The rest of the wolves did the same, going in different directions.

"Eric."

"Here, Ronni."

"Set up here for now. If anybody comes out of there, they don't go back, and they don't go home."

"Understood."

"Victor, you're our inventor and handyman, how do I get past the wire, both on the window and on her body?"

"We have wire cutters in the toolbox, can you carry them?"

"Show me."

He rummaged in the car for a moment then surfaced with a set of wire cutters. He grinned as he showed them to Rhonda. "Yes, I can carry those, and Justine as well."

"So, we're going in?" asked Justine.

"Yes. I don't want to wait for the wolves. Oh gods, Justine, she's so hurt."

"Keep it together, Lady Hawk. We'll get her out. How do you want to do this?"

Rhonda sucked in a deep breath to steady herself. "Eric, if the wolves find you a way in, use it. Clear the building. If they can't, stay here and make sure none escape. Peter, you and Victor hold this roadway if Eric leaves. We dare not let any of these people escape.

"Victor, I'll transform and land on the hood of the car. Once Justine has a tight grip on my leg, push the wire cutters into my talons. Make sure I have a good grip."

He nodded as she transformed and flew up then returned to land on the car. He knelt down and extended his arm. Justine's coat floated to the ground as she shimmered into the mouse and climbed onto his hand. He lifted her up then set her beside the hawk. She clambered onto the hawk's leg and squeaked once as she gripped that leg tightly.

Victor pushed the cutters into the hawk's talons, then lifted her gently and launched her skyward. A few beats of powerful wings and she was away toward the brightly lit castle. Rhonda climbed higher, then circled around to the back of the structure. Carefully, she landed so the mouse and the wire cutters wouldn't fall.

She then transformed but couldn't hold her grip and she fell away toward the jagged rocks far below. The mouse squeaked in terror as Rhonda fell, but she saw as the woman became the hawk in mid-fall. The fall turned into a glide, then a few beats of her wings later she was back at the window ledge. This time she got a tight hold on the wire mesh as she changed.

Shivering in the cold, and swearing like mad, the naked woman seized up the wire cutters and began to snip away at the offending barrier. A few snips and she was able to bend the wire inward enough for the mouse to get through. "The camera, Justine. Disable the damn camera." The mouse squeaked then wriggled through and into the cell.

Rhonda was shivering harder in the cold night air, her hands shaking as she continued to work away at the offending wire. Justine finished disabling the camera as Rhonda pushed the wire further open, shoved the wire cutters through to clatter to the floor, then fell away from the window.

Gudrun watched with a racing heart as the mouse scampered down the door frame and across the floor to morph into a woman who scooped up the wire cutters. The hawk reappeared at the window and pushed her way through to swoop towards her, shimmering into Rhonda.

Tears flowing freely, Rhonda cradled Gudrun's head gently, kissing her forehead and bloodied lips. "Easy, my sister, easy. We'll get you out of here. Justine, cut the strap on this damned gag first." The strap parted to the cutter blades and Rhonda ever-so-gently worked the gag out of Gudrun's mouth.

Gudrun's parched lips moved painfully, but no sound came out. "I know, honey, I know. You need blood. Just give us another minute, we'll get you fixed up, I promise." Justine worked carefully until the wire bindings were completely gone. Gently, she helped Rhonda straighten Gudrun's arms and legs.

"Blood. Need blood."

The voice was barely a whisper. "My god, she's so hurt, so weak."

"Keep it together, Ronni. What's the next move?"

"You'll have to pull her off me before she kills me."

"What? Ronni, you can't ..."

Justine's warning came too late. Rhonda had already lifted Gudrun's mouth to her neck. "Do it, sister, bite me." Gudrun didn't respond, she was too far gone, she couldn't extend her fangs.

"Shit." Rhonda winced as she bit her own wrist enough to make it bleed. She pushed the wound to Gudrun's battered lips and a moment later felt the soft tongue licking at the blood. Soon she gasped as she felt Gudrun shift to her neck, the fangs pierce her skin, and the vampire begin to suck greedily.

"That's enough," said Justine, after the vampire'd had a few moments to feed. She pulled hard at Gudrun's shoulders. "Stop, you're killing her. Stop now, goddamnit. Here, take some of mine now."

"No," said Gudrun, as she thrust Rhonda away. Her eyes were afire with the blood lust, but she was managing. "No, not you, either of you, but I need more."

Rhonda groaned and sat back up. "Justine, there should be a guard or two nearby, see if you can get somebody's attention."

"Working." She rose and went to the door, pulling it open. "Hey out there, anybody got a warm coat they'd be willing to share?" She couldn't understand the language, but she understood the intent as she backed away from the man with the gun. He was signaling for her to turn around and bend over.

His eyes were locked on Justine's naked form. She'd moved away so he had his back to Gudrun and Rhonda. Gudrun was terribly weak still, but Rhonda had regained her feet. She stepped up behind the man and tapped him on the shoulder. As he spun around, Justine's fist cracked against his jaw, and he melted toward the floor. Justine dragged him over to Gudrun.

He regained consciousness in time to see the vampire extend her fangs. Her hand managed to stifle his screams as she bit deep into his neck and drank greedily. He fought for a few moments, but soon went limp in her grip. She drank until there was no more to be had.

Rhonda and Justine watched as the vampire's tormented body magically began to heal itself and she rose in full killing mode. When she spoke she was Gudrun the Warrior once again. "You two are freezing to death. Ronni, can you carry Justine to safety?"

"Oh hell no, I can barely stand. I'll need a bit of time."

"Transform then, remain here and stay as warm as you can."

"Gudrun, the wolves are trying to find another way in. If they can, Eric and the crew will be coming through."

"Understood." With that, she silently faded through the door. They soon heard the screams and gunfire outside.

"Grab that guy's coat, I'll go hawk and you can tuck it around me then go mouse and I'll snuggle you under my wing. That should keep us warm."

"Works for me." Justine began working the dead guard's coat off him. "Ronni, you're the craziest person I've ever known. You find a weakened vampire and the first thing you do is feed her your own blood."

"You should talk, you were ready to feed her yourself."

Justine chuckled as she finally pulled the heavy wool coat free of the corpse. "Does that mean I'm as crazy as you?"

"Sadly, dear, it does. Now tuck me in then come snuggle with me while our sister goes on a killing rampage."

"Yeah, sure can't blame her for that, the bastards had her trussed with razor wire. If I wasn't so damn cold I'd go help her." She put the coat around the hawk then morphed into the mouse and scampered into the coat with Rhonda, snuggling under her wing.

Wolves

The wolves moved swiftly through the forest, eyes, ears, and nose searching everywhere. While Rhonda fed Gudrun her life's blood, Nikka found the bolt hole. Someone had recently gone out through. She threw back her head and gave a long howl, then shimmered back into the young woman.

Igor was the first to reach her, but only by seconds. "There." She said, as she pointed out the narrow tunnel. "There's a fresh scent. Someone has recently come out through."

"Are you sure they didn't go in?" asked Illya.

"No, I can smell the fear, and the tracks in the mud go away, besides, why would someone going in use the tunnel and not the road?"

"She's right," grinned Igor. "Wolves, we go after that one. Nikka. Find Eric and bring him here. Go through with him in case he needs you. Come, we go." He morphed back into the wolf and set out, following the scent Nikka had found. The others went with him, and she turned back to locate Eric.

She found him behind a pile of boulders, a perfect sniper's nest. "Eric, I've found the way in. Igor said to take you there."

Eric gave a soft whistle and both Jimmy and Vassily popped up from their hiding places. Eric nodded to Nikka, waved at his men, then followed her into the trees. By the time they reached the tunnel they could hear gunfire from the castle.

Nikka started into opening, but Eric called her back, winked at her as he donned the night vision goggles, then led the way in. They soon reached a set of stairs that climbed upwards. Emerging from the tunnel into a small cell that looked like an office, Eric swept off the goggles and stepped cautiously to the door. The others were already in the room behind him.

Gunfire and screams could be heard from outside. Eric eased open the door and stepped through. An older man fleeing toward him skidded to a halt, but Eric's fist sent him to the floor, unconscious.

Eric ran up a flight of stairs and reached an open courtyard. The battle was in full swing now. Gudrun was there, moving at terrible speed, but there were too many of them for her and she was slowing down. She took more hits, and a heavy net dropped over her even as the man in her grip screamed, her fangs biting deeply into his neck.

Several men began to converge on her, but a wolf shot past Eric and tore into one man. The others stopped in confusion for only a heartbeat, but it was enough. Gudrun's crew opened fire and seconds later the enemy was down.

They raced to Gudrun and pulled the heavy net off her. "They're using tranquilizers," she gasped, as she struggled to get to her feet. "I need some live ones to question. I need more blood, that or I'll have to sleep for a week while this crap wears off."

"I'll find you a fresh one," grinned Eric. "Nikka, stay with her, Jimmy too." He and Vassily began a sweep of the structure.

Nikka transformed and helped Gudrun to her feet. "Where is the Lady Hawk and Justine?"

"They're safe, little sister. I was so far gone, Ronni fed me her own blood. She was too weak to fly so they're still in the cell where I was held. They're probably frozen by now. Go to them, help them. Down the stairs over there, turn right, follow the scent. You'll find them. Jimmy can keep me company."

Nikka nodded then shimmered into the wolf and trotted away. Grinning, Jimmy passed Gudrun a bottle of blood and winked at her. She popped the stopper out and took a long drink. She sighed and gave his arm a tight squeeze. "This was a close one, Boss."

"Too close, Jimmy. As soon as I get clear-headed again I'm going after those bastards."

"As far as I know, only one got away. Igor and the wolves are on his trail right now."

"No, there's more, a whole network of them. Damn that Mobutu to hell."

"Mobutu?"

"It was one of his killing sprees that started this." She sighed as she drained the bottle and leaned against the cold stone. Eric and Vassily soon returned herding five men ahead of them. Nikka was right behind them with Rhonda and Justine, both dressed in the warm coats of the dead guards.

"Sit there," said Nikka. "Your feet must be frozen by now. Put your toes in my fur and warm up until Peter gets here with your clothes." They sat as she transformed and, smiling, wriggled their toes into her warm fur.

Gudrun pushed herself away from the wall, grabbed one of the prisoners, extended her fangs and bit him. He screamed and fought, but to no avail. She took what she needed then thrust him away. He sat whimpering as she walked over to Rhonda.

Rhonda looked up as the smiling vampire approached and sat beside her. Putting her arms around the Lady Hawk's shoulders, Gudrun kissed her forehead. "You are without doubt the craziest and most dear woman I've ever known, Lady Hawk. Bite me? Seriously?"

Rhonda giggled. "Seemed like a good idea at the time."

"I owe you my life, my sister. If there's ever anything I can do ..."

"There is, Gudrun, there is. I know I've driven you mad in the past, but that was the past. I need you to teach me everything you can."

"I will, Ronni. I will, I promise."

"Eric, are we clear?"

"We're clear, Lady Hawk. One managed to escape, but Igor and the wolves went after him."

"Fair enough. Call Peter and have him bring up the vehicles and some warm socks." Eric chuckled as he reached for his phone.

A few minutes later they heard the rumbling of engines and two of the cars appeared. Rhonda was still pulling on her clothes as she continued issuing orders. Gudrun grinned as she watched the Lady Hawk take command.

"Gudrun's still groggy and beat up. Jimmy, warm up a car for her. Do you need more blood?" Gudrun shook her head, so Rhonda turned to Peter. "Peter, you and Victor interrogate these men. Use the compulsion on them, learn all you can of what was to happen here, and the extent of their organization if they have one.

"Nikka, get Justine into a car and warm her up. Our poor little mouse has earned her keep this night. Oh, see if you can find me something to eat, would you?"

"Right here, Lady Hawk," said Vassily, as he passed her a protein bar and a concentrated liquid meal.

"Thanks, Vassily, you're a life saver. Now to report to the king." She found her phone in her pocket and called. It was answered on the first ring.

"Harald."

"Ronni here, Sire. Success. We have Gudrun back and she's recovering nicely. Igor and the wolves are still out after a fugitive."

"Wonderful news, Lady Hawk. Come home as soon as you can."

"As soon as we tidy this up we'll come home."

"There's more to do?"

"Yes. As soon as Gudrun is recovered I want to confer with her, learn what happened, see if there are more loose ends to deal with..."

"Ronni, easy girl. You do what must be done. Let us know if there's anything I can do from this end."

"I will, Sire. Oh, Harald, I should tell you, my husband went super alpha all over Illya and now controls all the werewolves."

"Sally warned me to expect that one day. Thanks for the heads up. Well done, Lady Hawk, wrap this up and come home."

"As soon as possible, Sire."

"So, you're the woman in charge here?" grinned Gudrun.

"Yeah. It's all Igor's fault, he made me do it."

"Did he say why?"

"Yeah, he did. Queen Sally's been having visions of a distant future."

"And?"

"And in those vision, I'm the queen, you, Victor, and Ella are my companions and advisors, and I have an army of werewolves, thousands of them. Igor bought into it and went ape shit all over Illya, taking control of all the wolves, setting that part in motion. Worse yet, Harald has gone all big brother on me."

Gudrun grinned and hugged her shoulders tighter for a moment. "I think you like it."

"Yeah, I like him trying to mentor me, but I don't want his job, Gudrun. I'll play along, but he's the man with the experience and know how to keep us all safe, not me.

"Poor Terry had a meltdown, Sally got a quick vision, and next thing you know I'm flinging orders like a drill sergeant."

"Ah, you enjoyed it," giggled Justine.

"That's the scary part. I'm afraid I might like it too much. Look, girls, if Harald starts making me lead more missions, I'll need you to keep me grounded. Igor won't do it, but I know you two can and will. Promise me now, if it starts going to my head, remind me I made you promise."

"Count on it," grinned Justine.

Gudrun didn't respond, she just snuggled down onto Rhonda's shoulder. "They were using tranquilizer loads," said Eric. "That's probably how they took her down in the first place."

"Yeah, she'll have to sleep it off, I guess. Get her in the warm car now, guys."

Eric gently lifted Gudrun in his arms then put her in the back seat of the warm car, climbing in with her to hold her gently. She settled against his shoulder, allowing the sleep to claim her.

Rhonda turned to Peter who was approaching. "We've questioned those men, Lady Hawk. They're members of a group, a secret society of vampire hunters. The old man was a close friend to the leader, but the man fled and left him behind when you set Gudrun free. With luck, Igor will have caught him."

"Is it ever that easy, Peter?"

He chuckled at that. "Not in recent memory, no."

"Are they all under the compulsion?"

"Yes."

"Bring the leader's buddy to me. Tell him he must speak only the truth to me, obey my every command, and then release him from the compulsion to remain still." Grinning, Peter returned to the captives. She smiled as she heard that deep bass voice give the man his marching orders.

Peter soon returned with the old man. "This woman is Lady Hawk. You will be serving her as she chooses."

"Of course," he replied, as he gave Rhonda a formal bow.

"What's your name?"

"I am Melosh, Lady, at your service."

"Tell me, Melosh, how did your people become aware of vampires?"

"It was long ago, Lady. I was a young man then, and Johan was a mere boy. Several families had gathered at the church for a wedding celebration. A stranger was there, a dark man with a jagged scar on his face. As the festivities began he stepped outside, then the creatures came.

"It was horror beyond belief. They killed and killed, drinking the blood, slashing and clawing at their victims. The man with the scar laughed and laughed as he watched, then he killed the monsters and walked away. He had not noticed the boy in hiding, watching as he tortured the child's mother. As he walked away he set the place afire and left us there to die.

"I was lying beneath several dead bodies, but still drew breath. When he was gone I crawled out, took the boy, and he helped me bind my wounds and escape that place. I raised him as my own and we studied the vampire, devised a way to catch and kill one.

"However, it has taken long years to find one, and then only by accident. The men wanted to kill her right there, but Johan insisted we bring her here, return the torment that was visited upon us."

"How did you find her? How did you capture her?"

"It was pure chance, Lady. We were on our way here for a training exercise with the men. We stopped for food and drink. As we were leaving we saw a man drag a woman into an alley. We hurried after them to rescue her, but as we arrived we saw her change and we knew. Johan and I were closest, so we grabbed the tranquilizer rifles and opened fire.

"The other men brought the nets and the wire. Once the drugs had her weakened, Johan bound her with the wire so she couldn't escape. As soon as he had the gag in her mouth we took off the hearing protection, threw her in the truck, and brought her here."

Gudrun's voice sounded right behind him. "Which one is Johan?"

"He escaped, left me to face the other vampire." He was trying to hide behind Rhonda, but she grabbed him and thrust him out to face Gudrun.

"What other vampire?"

"Your mate. He saw in your eyes that you no longer feared him. We knew your mate was here to rescue you."

Rhonda could see Gudrun was fighting to hold herself in check. "Gudrun, my sister, this man was the mentor and personal aide of the man who tortured you. He also knows how and where to find the others in the network, don't you, Melosh?"

"Yes, Lady Hawk."

"I need him alive for the moment. Right now you need to go home, fully recover, then come back to me."

"Ronni?"

"We had to sedate Terry. He needs to see you, hold you in his arms, and you need that too. Go home to him, recover, then rejoin me at Peter's sanctuary. Igor's claimed those wolves as well and will want to spend a few days with them to reinforce that bond.

"I need that time with Melosh to gain all the knowledge he has of this vampire hunting network. When you return we'll take up the hunt together, put an end to this."

"Ronni?"

"Gudrun, please trust me here. This is personal for you, and it is for me too. They hurt my sister, and they'll pay for that, but we need to look at the big picture also. These people could expose our existence; we dare not allow that. You go, comfort your husband, then come back to me ready for war."

"You've changed, Lady Hawk," said Gudrun, as she hugged Rhonda gently. "I think I like it. You're in command here; I'll do as you say, for I can feel Terry now. You're right, he needs me. Just make sure these bastards don't escape."

"We'll hunt them all down together, my sister, every damn one of them, even if it takes generations, we'll finish this properly. Go on now, but don't wait too long to come back." She kissed Gudrun's cheek and passed her to Eric. She was still struggling with the drug in her system.

"Eric, you guys take her home as fast as you safely can. Igor and I'll go back with Peter. Leave the car and we'll pick it up on the way by." Eric gave her the nod of approval as he helped Gudrun back into the car, Jimmy and Vassily close behind.

"Lady Hawk, what of these men?" asked Peter, as they watched Eric drive away.

"Use the compulsion, have them pile the dead bodies in the hidden tunnel. Victor, can you cause the tunnel to cave in?"

"I can, Lady Hawk, and I will. What of these men, do we kill them and place them in the tunnel as well?"

All eyes turned to Rhonda. She didn't speak for several long moments, then her eyes hardened. "Yes." Peter nodded, then he and Victor went to the captives and soon they were gathering up the bodies of the dead.

Justine reached out to lightly grip Rhonda's arm. "Is it really necessary to kill them, Ronni?"

"They knew what that bastard was doing to her. They heard her screams, yet they did nothing to stop him. They were here to protect him while he killed her slowly, they protected him as he tortured her. We're no longer human, Justine, but these bastards are the ones who're inhumane.

"We'll use the vampire's compulsion on the rest of the network as we find them, but not these. This is the line in the sand. You torture one of my people, you pay the price. When we find this Johan, Gudrun will deal with him herself.

"So, disappointed in me, J?"

"No, I get it, Ronni, I do. You're right here. You'd better check in with the king while the boys get things organized."

Rhonda nodded and pulled out her phone again. "Harald here. Rhonda, all is well?"

"All good here, Sire. I've sent Gudrun home with her crew; she needs a day or two to rest and to see Terry. After that I need her back here ready for war. I've got the second-in-command of the vampire hunter's network. I'll get what information I can from him, then start to hunt and shut them down. Gudrun will want to be here for that, and I do want her with me on that hunt.

"Right now I'll take Igor back to Peter's sanctuary so he can bond with the new pack. That'll give me time to gather information and lay plans."

She could hear the smile in his voice as he replied. "Sounds to me like you've got things well in hand, Ronni. All right, Lady Hawk,

I'll put all our resources available to you for this. You understand this network must be utterly silenced."

"I do, Harald. I'm fully aware of what we have at stake here. Do you want to take charge of this personally? Put Gudrun in charge, perhaps?"

"No, not really. You seem to have a handle on it. Use whatever means necessary, Ronni, but get this done."

"As you desire, my king." He was chuckling as she broke the connection.

"Here comes Igor," said Nikka.

A moment later the wolves entered the courtyard and transformed. "Igor?"

"Whoever he was, he escaped us, my pretty bird. There was a hidden vehicle, and it was gone before we could run him down. Do we know who it was? Tell me it wasn't the leader."

"It was the leader," she sighed. "As soon as Victor collapses the tunnel on the dead bodies we'll go back to the sanctuary with them. You need time with your new pack, and I need time to crawl through Melosh's memories."

"Who is Melosh?"

"The leader's foster father, his close companion, and his fellow planner. Ah, here comes Peter now."

Peter returned with Victor and Melosh. "It's done, Lady Hawk."

"I didn't hear any explosion."

"You will," grinned Victor. Right on cue there was an explosion that rocked the ground. "And there you go."

"Victor, you're the best," grinned Rhonda. "All right, people, we're done here. Peter, take us home. Igor and I'll be your house guests for a few days."

"It will be our pleasure, Highness."

Rhonda turned to gaze open-mouthed at him. "What did you just call me?"

"Sorry."

"Peter, what did you mean by that?"

"Lady Hawk, it is quite plain to me that Harald is planning to make you his heir. Highness is proper address for a princess." Rhonda just groaned, rolled her eyes, and climbed into the car.

"I'm not a princess yet, I'm just a gal who need a rare steak and a bottle of red wine."

Peter grinned at that. "Bring up the blood? You fed Gudrun, didn't you?"

"Yeah, I did. It was the only way; she was so weak."

"There was another option."

"You mean kill her and wait for her to revive? I couldn't, Peter, I just couldn't. She's one of us, they'd hurt her so badly, and the idea of bringing more harm to her ... I just couldn't."

"I believe Harald has chosen well," smiled Peter, as he turned onto the highway to Imatra and the Russian border beyond.

Revived

The plane came in low and fast, banked once, then settled to the ground. A group of people were waiting to greet them, and Gudrun's husband was first in line as she descended from the aircraft. She leaped into his waiting arms. "Terry. Oh, my darling Terry."

Tears ran freely down his face as he hugged her tightly. "Dammit, Blondie, why can't you ever stay out of trouble?"

"Beat me up later, lover. Right now I'm still full of tranquilizer and need to report to the king."

"You need rest, Gudrun," smiled Harald. "It can wait."

"No, it can't, Sire. We have to do this while it's still fresh in my mind."

"Then bring her to the great hall, Terry. We'll get this done then she can rest and sleep it off."

A few short moments later they were in the great hall, as were many of the lair's folk. Terry gently lowered Gudrun into a chair then sat close to her. The king took his queen's hand in his then nodded.

Gudrun shook her head to clear away some of the cobwebs. Sitting up straighter, she began her report. "I was captured and tortured by a couple of madmen, humans who survived one of Mobutu's killing sprees. Two humans survived that horror, a man and a boy.

"The man took the boy and raised him. Together they studied everything they could about vampires, torture, and more, and then plotted their revenge. That boy grew to a man studying methods of inducing pain, studying, and practicing. Who knows how many he's tortured to death as he explored the ways to confine and control a creature much stronger than himself.

"The bastard escaped, but his mentor and constant companion wasn't so lucky. I was listening as the Lady Hawk interrogated the old man. This is what I learned. They've recruited and trained a network of vampire hunters.

"By a stroke of mischance, they saw a man drag me into an alley and ran to my rescue. One glance at me feeding and they opened fire with tranquilizer guns which they always carry. They believe bullets to be useless, besides they wanted a specimen to study before killing it. I was elected.

"The drug slowed me down enough for the nets to be thrown over me. The voice of command was useless as they'd donned hearing protection. Once I was subdued, a gag was forced into my mouth so I couldn't speak, and I was bound with razor wire so any struggle or attempt to transform brought intense pain and damage to my body.

"They often came to torment me, testing my healing powers, and enjoyed gloating as they beat or cut me. He, the leader, promised many times that, at the end, he would cut off my head and throw it into the sea while his companion cremated the body."

She paused there to let all that sink in. Jimmy passed Gudrun a bottle of blood and she gave him a weak smile of thanks as she drank deeply. She then took up the story again.

"He told me I would be kept alive until the anniversary of the day Mobutu killed his mother, then I'd be put on display for the whole network and slain. That day was fast approaching, and I was so weak; I'd given up hope and was saying my goodbyes in my mind when I felt it, another vampire drawing near.

"I lay still, not daring to hope, when I felt the second vampire and knew them. It was Victor and Peter. Hope rose up in me, and then I saw the hawk at the window. I knew then that Igor and the wolves would be with them.

"The Lady Hawk flew off, but soon returned with a mouse and wire cutters. Together Rhonda and Justine cut me free, but I was too far gone, couldn't even extend my fangs. Ronni cut herself and gave me the blood until I could feed myself. She pressed me to her neck and fed me.

"Justine managed to pull me off in time, then she lured a guardsman into the cell, knocked him unconscious and dragged him over to me to feed on and renew myself.

"Half mad with the thirst and the killing lust, I went at them, but they were too many and using tranquilizers again. I'd left Justine caring for the weakened Lady Hawk and was down again when Eric and the boys arrived to save my ass.

"That brings me to now, Ronni will be able to give you the rest. She has the old man and is taking him to the Russian sanctuary for further interrogation."

King Harald sighed as he relaxed back into his chair. "This is truly distressing news, but we've always known this could happen. I've heard from Rhonda, and she believes we still have time to shut this down, but she wants you with her."

"Forgive me, Harald, but I get the impression our young and wild Lady Hawk has risen in your estimation. Are you planning to make her the heir?"

"I am. Gudrun, tell me how you feel about this."

"I will confess that at one point, since Mother doesn't seem to want the job, I did see myself as the most likely candidate for the task."

"But now?"

"She found me, Harald, and she found a way to get through the barriers to free me. She fed me her own blood. Yes, the Lady Hawk is wild and impetuous, but I'm hers now, forever. Do it, promote her. I swear I'll serve her as loyally as I do you."

"Thank you, Gudrun. That does ease my mind. As I said, I've spoken with her and, as impatient as she is to get on the trail of this madman, she's agreed to wait until I send her a team to help her. I didn't tell her, but I'm sending her a special team."

"Special team?"

"Yes, Gudrun. You and Ella. Take Terry and your men as well, but I want both of you with her."

"Just what are you up to, my king?"

"Sally has had a number of visions of a distant future, Gudrun."

"Oh?"

"Yes," smiled the queen. "In those visions, everything is different, sometimes war, others peace, some happy, some intense, but three things are always the same. Rhonda is queen, you, Ella, and Victor are always at her side, and she is worshiped by an army of werewolves."

Gudrun looked sadly at Harald, but he just chuckled. "I'm not dead yet, my sister. Go that far into the future and I've probably abdicated in favor of a younger and more energetic monarch. Sally hasn't seen my fate, Gudrun, only you four."

"Igor has already taken control of the wolves, so that part has already begun," sighed Gudrun, as she leaned on Terry's shoulder. "So has the rest, I guess, for I'm hers, no question."

"Goody, what aren't you telling us?" asked Terry.

"She marked me, Terry." The whole room went quiet at that. "Oh, she didn't mean to do it, nor did she know it would happen, nobody did. I was all torn up, ripped half apart, blood from head to toe. She cradled me in her arms, kissed me, then fed me her blood.

"She must have gotten a taste of my blood when she kissed me. I felt it as I drank of her, but couldn't stop. As Justine pulled me off she too offered her blood, but I pushed her away, not wanting that connection with her too.

"Rhonda is immortal as we are, and the bond created here was different as well. She always calls me her sister, and I have tried to play that role for her, but now that's what we are. As I felt the bond, I also felt it pushed back at me by the power of her personality.

"She turned it back on me, the brat. She now knows that I'll serve her forever, but I know the reverse is true as well. The eternal soldier and the Lady Hawk are truly sisters now, utterly devoted to each other for all time. Even now I can feel her, her restlessness, her love for Igor, her devotion to you, Harald, to all the non-humans. No, Sire, you have chosen wisely."

She was nearly asleep on Terry's shoulder now. "Take her away, Terry, put her to bed. When she awakens all will be ready for the trip to Russia."

"Sire ..."

"Yes, I want you to go with her. Go on now, take her to her rest."

In the Sanctuary

The car bumped along, and the constant rocking motion lulled Rhonda into a near sleep as she cuddled in Igor's arms. They stopped for breakfast in Imatra, drawing plenty of interest. So many foreigners at this time of year was unusual. Victor and Peter ordered for them and did all the talking.

The food seemed to revive the Lady Hawk somewhat, and she began to take a greater interest in the world around her as they headed for the Russian border. Peter worked his magic again and they were soon through and headed for the sanctuary.

Once off the highway, the road was somewhat rougher and once again Rhonda snuggled down for a nap. She awakened when the vehicle suddenly stilled, and the engine went silent. They were inside a compound surrounded by a tall wire fence. It looked old, rarely used, more like a prison than a military base. She remarked upon it.

"You have a good eye, Lady Hawk. It's been used as both at one point in time or another. This was one of the old Soviet Union's guard stations, established to prevent people from defecting, as well as acting as a prison. It was abandoned when the wall fell, and we acquired it a number of years ago, in case we should ever need a place to retreat to. That was before Mobutu's last rampage. We Russians can sometimes be a little paranoid."

"Even paranoids can have enemies," she replied, as she patted his arm. "My question is, are you too remote here to feed yourselves?"

"We are, but we do have resources, many villages, dozens of cities in Finland, plus we have deliveries from Gudrun's blood bank in Moscow."

"She owns a blood bank?"

"Oh yes, several in the large cities of Europe. Most of it is delivered to different medical institutions, but some is diverted for our use."

"We also go to the cities of Finland regularly for our resident mouse," grinned Victor.

"Okay, I'm a shopaholic," said Justine, as Rhonda arched an eyebrow at her. "I admit it. The boys take me to the city, they hunt, I shop, it works."

Rhonda was laughing now. "So I see. You seem happy here, Justine. I'm pleased about that."

"Come," said Peter, "let me show you around inside. We've left the outside looking much as it has always done, but we've managed to update the inside." He led them into the main building and Rhonda gave a small cry of delight.

The inside was as modern as the outside was abandoned looking. Rhonda enjoyed her tour, as well as meeting Heinrich, the resident techno wizard. He seemed to have an eye for Justine, and Rhonda smiled at that. The super mouse didn't seem to mind at all.

"I'm afraid our guest quarters aren't as elegant as those of the Lair," said Peter, as he showed Rhonda and Igor to a well-appointed room.

"I like it," said Igor. "No windows to fall out of. Feels like a sweet den."

"Get some rest," smiled Peter. "Her Highness is nearly asleep on her feet."

With that he left them. Igor gently stripped off Rhonda's clothes and tucked her into the bed. "Hey there, tall dark and furry, where do you think you're going?"

"You rest now, my pretty bird. I have a new pack to attend to."

"That can wait, get naked and get in here, snuggle me to sleep. That was a royal command."

Igor chuckled as he stepped out of his clothes. "Yes, my pretty princess, I hear and obey." He slipped under the covers with her and took her into his arms. He kissed her softly then snuggled her down onto his shoulder. She was instantly asleep.

They emerged hours later to find a woman in a chair outside their door, reading. She glanced up and smiled, then stood and gave them a slight bow. "I'm Lidiya, your Highness. With permission I'll lead you to the dining room. Miss Justine and Nikka are already there."

At Rhonda's nod she turned and walked away. They followed closely and were in a large dining room. As Rhonda entered everyone stopped eating and stood up, only resuming their seats once Igor had her settled in a chair beside Justine. "That was weird."

"Get used to it, Ronni," grinned Justine. "You're royalty now."

"The hell I am."

"I have it on good authority you soon will be. We've received word there will soon be a gathering of the non-humans at the Lair, the king is going to officially announce his heir. That's you, by the way. God, first you steal my guy, then you take over the world. What's next on the list?"

"Well, next week I thought I'd conquer the universe, want to come with me?"

"Love to. Ronni, in all honesty, I'm pleased for you. I saw you in action the past few days and I think the king's made the right decision. I know what you have to do over the next while. I'll admit, I'm no detective, nor a warrior, but whatever you need from me, I'll be there."

"Thanks, honey. We did make a heck of a team, didn't we?"

"Yes we did, but next time can we do it in the summer? August maybe?"

"Still cold?"

"You know it."

"Maybe Heinrich could warm you up," grinned Rhonda.

"Mmm, now there's a thought. Igor, what do you think? Hey, where are you going?"

Red-faced, he sighed and kissed Rhonda's cheek. "I must spend the day with my wolves, Miss Justine." With that he walked away to the sound of Rhonda and Justine's laughter.

"The girls giving you trouble, Igor?" asked Peter, as he met Igor leaving the dining room. He'd obviously overheard and was enjoying the young man embarrassment.

"Da. Miss Justine's been gone from the Lair for over a year and still she gets me in trouble. I will go hide in the forest with the wolves." Peter's deep chuckle followed him through the door.

Outside in the open compound, Igor found the pack waiting for him. He shimmered into the wolf and raced into the trees, the entire pack following close behind. Silently they hunted, eventually crossing the trail of an elk. They swiftly ran down and killed the prey, Igor making the kill and taking the first meat, then standing back so the pack could feed.

When all had eaten their fill, he led then back to the stream they'd crossed, giving them water. He then sought out a clearing, transforming into the man and relaxing in the sun and cold bracing air. At a signal from his hand they all transformed to hear him speak.

"My people, I am alpha now, are there any challenges?" There were none. "My wolves, hear me, I will soon be returning to the west, leaving Illya as my second to lead you. My brothers and sisters, the great queen Sally has had visions of the future. In her visions there are werewolves, many thousands of werewolves, hundreds of packs. We will not perish and disappear; Stephan Krebs will not have made an end of us; the wolves will survive and thrive.

"People, the visions tell us how this comes to pass. In all the visions, the werewolves serve a single alpha, a queen, the Lady Hawk. This is why I have come to you, to tell you of these things, to make certain this is understood, that through all the generations, wolves must serve the Lady Hawk, all the alphas of all the packs must swear to this, all pups must be raised to know this. Only by her guidance will the wolves survive and grow stronger.

"I will now show you what the vampire queen has seen." He dropped to one knee and raised his right arm, closed fist, into the air. "Hail Lady Hawk, Hail the Queen!"

Igor rose to his feet, and with a shy smile, gazed at the people who were mostly his elders. "My friends, brothers and sisters, we must do this. The king will soon name the Lady Hawk as his heir. She is rising high, and growing much stronger, learning leadership from the king himself. She will lead us, protect us, and we will serve her without question.

"Now, after all I've said, I will listen to objections, or answer questions." There were none. Illya transformed and approached Igor, dropping into a submissive position. The others followed suit. Igor nodded his approval then shimmered into the wolf and led them back to the compound.

Peter and Rhonda were just stepping out the door as the wolves came racing into the yard. They came to Rhonda and when Igor transformed, the pack transformed. They all dropped to one knee with fist raised high. "Hail Lady Hawk, Hail the Queen!"

"Dammit, Igor ..."

"Accept this, Rhonda. Become who you're destined to be."

Rhonda looked at him and sighed. "All right, Peter." She turned to the werewolves. "Thank you, my people. I accept you. Now, show me your forest." With that, she leaped into the air, transforming into the hawk and climbing into the sky. They shimmered back into a wolf pack and raced off into the trees again, streaming out behind their alpha while the hawk soared above them.

The pack ran to where they'd left the carcass of the elk. They held back, but Igor approached and stood waiting. Overhead, Rhonda sighed, she understood what he was doing, what she had to do. "Ah, hell, maybe it'll help bring up my blood again."

She dropped from the sky, spreading her wings at the last second, landing beside the kill. Still in hawk form, she tore off some of the meat and ate it. She then flew up to perch in a tree and keep watch while first Igor ate some, and then the rest of the pack. She had shared a kill with them, they were completely hers now.

They returned to the sanctuary an hour later to find Peter still waiting for them, holding up Rhonda's clothes. She swooped in and landed easily beside him, laughing with delight. "That was a lot of fun. Thank you, my wolves, my friends."

She began to pull on her clothes. "I have to get some work done now. Igor, I want you with me when I question Melosh. Put your pants on first." There was a round of laughter at that as the pack dressed themselves as well. Igor nodded to Illya, then followed Rhonda and Peter inside.

Peter led them into a small office that had once been a real interrogation room. "Use your compulsion on him, Peter. I don't want to take any chances."

"I understand, Rhonda. I'll be right back with our informant."

He left and Igor settled into a chair while the Lady Hawk paced. A few moments later, Peter returned with Melosh, Nikka right behind them. Rhonda raised an eyebrow at her, but the girl grinned and held up a recording device plus a pen and writing pad. "He can't write in English, Lady Hawk, but I need the practice."

Rhonda smiled and nodded then turned her attention to Melosh. "All right, let's begin with Johan, where would he go? What will he do now?"

"He will go to St. Petersburg. We have a training facility there."

"Describe it."

"It's in a warehouse at the waterfront. There are old tunnels beneath the city, and one leads there."

"Describe the training."

"We practice with the tranquilizer guns, we practice throwing the nets over excited fighting dogs, we capture bad people and practice tying the wire knots. We have books of anatomy, books about knots, pressure and pain points."

"Describe how you capture bad people," said Igor. Completely under the vampire's compulsion spell, the man did not speak or acknowledge Igor at all, his focus completely on Rhonda.

"Answer his question."

"Yes, Lady. We would go out into the city, or surrounding towns, enter the bars, watch for the brutal men, the bullies. When they left the building, we would shoot them with the tranquilizers, throw the nets over them, tie them with the wire then take them back to the training center. We then demonstrated the tying and torture techniques, filming them, and the results, for the others."

"These men you captured, did they survive?"

"No, for the demonstration to be effective they were properly tortured then beheaded as taught to us by the scar-faced vampire himself."

Rhonda fought to keep her stomach down, and to keep from ripping his head off. "Tell me of capturing the vampire in Finland."

"We were there on a training mission, looking for a capture. When we saw the man drag the woman into the alley, we went after him. Our original target was the man, but when we saw the vampire we acted swiftly, the training proved effective."

"How many vampires have you managed to capture?"

"She was the first and only one we ever found. She was the final proof we needed."

"Did you document her capture and torture?"

"Of course. Not the capture, but once we had her everything was recorded."

"Where is the information stored?"

"On the computer at the stronghold."

"Was any of it shared with anyone? Did any of it ever reach the internet?"

"No, Lady. We were waiting until after the execution. Johan wanted to edit and make a proper training film, plus he wanted to make a special film for the media."

"When he fled without you, did he take any of that information with him?"

"I don't believe so, Lady. He used the escape tunnel. I was between him and the computer station, he did not go past me before he disappeared."

"Where are those computers now?"

"I don't know."

"We have them, Lady Hawk," said Peter. "Heinrich is already stripping them of information. Melosh, there were five training facilities listed on that computer. Are there more?"

"No, only five."

"Are they manned at all times?" asked Rhonda, as she read the paper Igor passed to her.

"Yes, Lady. All personnel are listed on the computer, as are all the home addresses of the people, the safe houses as well. As a precaution, I kept the only list on computer, but Johan will have his book."

"His book?"

"He doesn't trust computers, he kept separate records in his journal, as well as records of the training and test results."

"Test results?"

"Yes. We tested how humans reacted to the tortures, so we would know if we had captured a vampire. They would react differently, and we needed to fully understand the difference."

There was a soft knock on the door. Peter answered and spoke briefly to a man outside, then returned. "Heinrich has gathered all the information from this man's computer, Lady Hawk. He's now forming it into a useful format for us. We'll soon have a list of names and addresses for you."

"Thank you, Peter, that'll save us a world of time. Melosh, do you know every person in the network personally?"

"Yes, Lady. Johan and I chose each one together. First we managed to fully convince the candidate of the existence of vampires, then we personally train them as hunters."

"And to this day Gudrun was the only vampire any of you actually caught, but you filmed the torture and killing of the bad men you caught, is that correct?"

"Yes, Lady, that is correct."

Rhonda smiled as he confirmed this for her. "Peter, perhaps your computer wizard could prepare some of this video evidence for the authorities. It was rather helpful of these men to record the torture and murder of their victims.

"I believe the police might be interested in investigating a few of these places, but first we have to capture this Johan and doctor his records of Gudrun's torment."

"What should we do with this one?"

"Oh, I have plan for him and his son. Keep him on ice for me until we have the other one. We'll take them and a few others from their network back to where we found Gudrun, then we'll stage something for the police to find, film of their death.

"These serial murders captured a woman to torture, but they caught the wrong woman. The woman they captured is the leader of an elite team of mercenaries. Her men located her and raided the hideout, freeing their leader and eliminating the two main perpetrators of the madness. The two madmen who believed in vampires will have met their fate at the hands of one of their human victims."

Peter grinned broadly. "I like it, Rhonda, truly I do. I'll just return Melosh to his cell until we need him."

She nodded and he led the enthralled man away. "Nikka, ask Heinrich to get a copy of that interview to the king, would you?"

"At once, Lady Hawk." She hurried from the room.

"Are you all right, my pretty bird?"

"Igor, listening to that man made me want to yak up my breakfast. So help me, there are days I hate humans."

He took her gently into his arms and kissed her forehead. "I understand, my beloved, I do. However, the madness that drove these two men was a burden they gained from Mobutu. He drove them as mad as he was, and so we continue to deal with his insanity. These two men I can understand, it is those who followed them, engaged in the torture and murder, those are the ones who deserve a slow death."

"Igor, take me outside, into the forest again. I need to clear my head and shake this off."

"Da, let's go, my pretty bird. A flight in the clear air will do you good." He startled a bit as she instantly transformed and perched on his forearm. With a chuckle he walked outside and launched her skyward.

Return of the Vampire

While Gudrun slept in her husband's arms, and the Lady Hawk shared a kill with her wolves, Johan sat staring at the wall, the men around him quietly waiting for him to speak. He had arrived the night before, but still hadn't spoken a word. With a deep sigh of regret, he turned to acknowledge them.

"We failed," he said. "We had her, completely, and we learned much from the time of interrogation. Silver is useless against them, so is the cross, and she actually enjoyed the holy water. They do bleed, feel pain, are warm of body, and have a heartbeat, so they are actually alive, not living dead. They can also heal at an alarming rate, but starve them of blood to drink and that power fades."

"What of the stake, bright sunlight?"

"I don't know, we didn't get to that before disaster struck."

"Disaster? What do you mean, disaster, and where is Melosh?"

"Melosh is dead, as are the rest now. Melosh died a hero's death. I went to her cell and tightened her bonds, made her scream, further weakening her ability to heal, but something was wrong, there was no longer fear in her eyes. Even as she cried out in pain, she was no longer afraid of me. There could be only one answer, her mate had found her and was coming, she could sense him.

"I ran back to warn the others, but the beast was already among us, there was no hope. Melosh pushed me to safety even as the vampire took him from behind. I alone escaped the carnage. I hid in a secret passage until he cut her loose, fed her on Melosh and the others, then took her away. Once they were gone, I came here." In truth, he had spent a full day hiding in his car, just outside the city.

An air of anxiety and fear filled the room. "So, what do we do now?" asked one of the men.

"Now we know much of what we wanted to know," said Johan. "We keep hunting. The next one we catch we try the stake, and then the sunlight. Even if those fail, as Melosh always said, cut off the head and nothing can survive."

"Keep hunting? Are you mad? They know about us now; they'll be watching for us."

"And so we become even more cautious. We caught one, our methods, our training, work perfectly. We will find others, and we will kill them, but first we must learn all we can about them. Know your enemy, that's the key to our eventual success."

"That didn't work out so well for you, did it?"

Johan sighed. "Da, we made a bad mistake. We know now, they can find each other over great distances. Next time we will move about, a day here, a day there, until we know what we need to know. After death do they vanish into dust, or is there a body to dispose of? Who knows? I told that one I would behead her and burn the body but cast the head into the sea. I saw true terror in her eyes then. I believe that would have been a final end of her.

"So, we lay low for a few more days, then we begin the hunt again. For now I need rest and time to mourn the death of Melosh, then we avenge him." He rose and went to the small guard room area where there were a few cots. He sank onto one and was soon asleep.

Back at the lunch area, one man stabbed out his cigarette. "I've got a bad feeling about this."

"What?" asked another.

"Always he tells us nothing, then we get a call from Ansel, they've actually caught one, he says. He was so excited I believed him. I also think it got away from them because they got careless, stupid. It's one thing to hang onto a man and enjoy his slow departure from life, but far too much risk with a vampire. Once they fully realized what they had, they should have killed it."

"Da, I agree with that, so what do we do now?"

"Now we watch him carefully. He and Melosh have too much on video, too much of what we've done. What if Melosh escaped and got to a hospital. The authorities would be called, evidence found ..."

"Wasn't that the idea, gather evidence of vampires, expose them to the world?"

"Da, but what evidence would be found? How many men have we used as we trained, and trained others to hunt the vampire? Was there any actual evidence of a real vampire? If so, what was it? Or was there nothing but film of Johan torturing a woman?

"You heard him, the holy water, silver, and the cross had no effect on her. Was she really a vampire or just some woman that sick bastard decided to torture? He said she was warm, had a heartbeat. I've got a bad feeling here, that's what I'm saying. They've kept too many secrets from us. We need to keep a close watch on him from now on."

The others nodded their agreement. The idea of what they would face if the police ever got their hands on the training videos terrified them. In truth, none of them had ever seen a vampire, and had no actual evidence of their existence. Perhaps it had all been a lie, the product of a tortured and twisted mind. Slowly, the horror of their position began to sink in.

"Well, I for one, will not stay," said one man, as he rose and tossed down his vodka. "They have too much information lying around. I'll go to the east, shave my beard, find a job and disappear into the masses of a new city. I won't stay here to be caught and executed." With that, he walked away.

Of the ten men in the training center, only two were left to Johan when he awakened, and they were watching his every move. Realizing what had happened, he tried to reason with them, but saw it wasn't working. Without warning, he shot them both then left the building, leaving behind two torture victims still encased in razor wire.

WHILE JOHAN ABANDONED his safe center, far to the west a vampire awakened, somewhat refreshed, and hungry. She popped the top off the bottle of blood that was at her bedside and drank it all. Smiling with delight, she turned to the man in the bed. He was grinning at her.

"You look like you're back and ready for action. It's good to see you in one piece, Blondie."

"I've warned you about calling me that before," she grinned, as she pounced on him. "Now you pay." She closed his mouth with a searing kiss, and he hugged her tightly to him, his hands exploring her body as though searching for evidence of the torment she'd endured.

"As you can see," she smiled, as their lips parted, "I'm good as new. Now stop poking around like a nurse and start poking around like a man who wants me."

Some time later, their passion sated for the moment, she lay in his arms, listening to his heartbeat. "Feeling better now?"

"Yeah, I am. Gods, I ..."

"Hey now, none of that. I'm all good, and now you have to help me get some payback."

"Right, we need to get to work, I guess. Do you think there's a chance we could slip away for a few weeks once this is done?"

"Are you serious? My workaholic husband wants to go on vacation?"

"I want to get you all to myself for a few weeks, someplace where you can't get into trouble."

She laughed and hugged him tightly. "We'll do it, Terry, I promise. First, we have work to do. Lady Hawk is getting restless. If we don't get a move on she'll start without us."

She rose from the bed with a liquid grace and pulled another bottle blood from the cupboard. She drained it, then turned to find him already dressed. "Hurry up, woman, we've got to get moving," he grinned. She threw a pillow at him then swiftly dressed.

WHILE TERRY JOINED Eric and the men for breakfast, Gudrun sought out Ella and the king. "Are you certain you're ready?" asked Harald, as she entered his study where Ella was waiting with him.

"I'm ready, Sire." She smiled as she sank into a chair facing him. "My body's recovered, and my mind is clear. This is a revenge hunt, yes, but more importantly, it's a hunt to ensure our continued anonymity. Revenge is secondary here, as in truth, it was Mobutu who sparked all this."

"How's your connection to Rhonda, now that you've recovered?"

"It's extremely strange, Harald, and yet comforting somehow. I can feel her now; restless, anxious to get started, and that urges me to hurry, to get to her, to be with her on the hunt, but it's so very different to the connection with Terry. You know how that one works, and the connection to Rhonda doesn't interfere with it."

"So she's in a hurry to get started, is she?" The king grinned like a proud father. "Perhaps that connection between you will help her be a bit more measured in her approach to the world. All right, ladies, I wish you god speed." In mere moments the plane lifted off and was on its way to Russia.

WHILE THE PLANE WAS in the air, Rhonda paced about the interrogation room; Igor sat patiently waiting. He wasn't offering any help, and she was getting irritated with it. "Come on, Igor, help me here."

"What do you want me to do, my pretty bird?"

"Stop patronizing me, stop sitting there like a two-year-old meadow muffin and help me, tell me what's our next move?"

"A two-year-old meadow muffin?" He grinned. "That's a bit harsh, isn't it?"

"Maybe, but you're pissing me off. You're the alpha, the take charge guy, the king's go-to agent, and you're just sitting there."

"I serve the queen of the werewolves. I am waiting for her to give me a task."

Tears of frustration leaked from her eyes as she glared at him. "Hug me, dammit, that's an order." She was instantly wrapped up in his loving arms, his kiss on her forehead, the warmth of his body and the sound of his heartbeat soothing, comforting her. "Igor, I'm doing my best here, but I need you to get in the game with me, help me."

"I'm trying to do just that, my beloved Lady Hawk. In the years to come you will have to do these things without me. Another will be here to advise you, and we are waiting for her to arrive."

"Dammit, Igor, you have to stop this. If you try to pull away from me I swear I'll pull out every chest hair you've got, one at a time. Yes, I'll need Gudrun's advice, her guidance, but I'll always have that. Our time together is finite. If I'm going to lead the werewolves into the future, I need you to teach me how to do that, everything there is to know about the wolves and how to help them.

"Do you understand? I need your guidance, especially about the wolves; Gudrun can't help me with that."

"I know, sweet Ronni, I know."

"So help me."

"My love, just tell me what you need, what are we discussing? Are we talking about the wolves, the vampires, all non-human folk, or the vampire hunters? Where are your thoughts focused?"

She sighed and pulled back to look into his eyes, seeing the love and devotion there. "So I'm too scattered and you were waiting for me to get focused on something, anything?"

"Da, that."

"I'm sorry, lover, I'm just so used to you doing it. You always give me a direction, and then I focus on that for you. Okay, I can do this. I'm queen of the werewolves, so I need to protect them, keep them safe.

Under the current circumstances, shutting down these vampire hunters will keep us all much safer, including the wolves. Let's focus there. So, what do I do?"

"Think like the wolf."

She pushed out of his arms. "Dammit to hell, Igor, if you don't stop this I'll transform and peck your tail off." She stopped ranting as she saw his eyes. "Oh my god, you're serious." He nodded silently.

"All right, think like the wolf. The wolf is a hunter. If the wolf hunts mice he does one thing, for rabbits another, and for an elk something different, why? Every prey is different, and the wolf knows his prey. That's the problem here, I know next to nothing about this prey.

"Okay, so, I need to learn more about this man I hunt. How do I do that? Melosh, I interrogate Melosh again." Igor's bright smile of approval told her she'd got it right. Rhonda grabbed him by the collar and pulled herself closer. "Listen you, I can take the tough teacher crap from Gudrun, but not you, I need you to be gentle with me, make me feel safe. I mean it Igor, no more of this crap."

"Was that a royal decree?"

"No, this is. Kiss me like you mean it then drag that evil bastard back here for me."

He held her gently and kissed her, holding the kiss until she melted against him. "I'm so sorry, my sweet Ronni," he breathed softly. "I didn't mean to upset you. I will try a different way."

"No, it's okay, lover. Just tell me when I get too scattered, remind me to focus, and then help me stay focused."

"I will, my pretty bird. Igor will bring the madman to you now. We will learn as much as we can about the enemy." He walked out, but soon returned with Victor and Nikka as well as Melosh.

Rhonda stood studying the old man who was still as stone while he waited for instruction. Finally she spoke. "I have questions for you, Melosh."

"Of course, Highness. I'm here to serve."

"Speak to me of Johan the boy, the child you rescued. What was he like? What things did he enjoy? You were a father to him, what sorts of things did he like to do?"

"Johan enjoyed very little, Lady. In the early days all he did was cry for his mother, and nothing could console him. I, too, was mourning the horrific deaths of my own family. Perhaps I could have done more for him.

"Nothing brought him joy, Lady. The stars were as close as he ever came. He would sneak outside to gaze at the night sky as he had often done with his mother. As he grew older he would speak to me of this. It was difficult at times."

"Difficult?"

"Yes, Lady, difficult to re-focus him on the holy quest. He would get lost in the mourning of his mother and forget about the need to avenge her, to utterly destroy the entire species of the vampire."

"Tell me more of this."

"When he was young he seemed to like the training, the trapping of animals, the learning of knots. He even seemed to enjoy their screams of pain as we practiced the knots with wire. As he grew to a man he began to doubt what we did. I had to change some of his training."

"Change how?"

"I took him to the house of a dangerous man. We sat outside listening as the man beat his wife. Listening to her screams brought Johan back to the task at hand. The next day we captured that man, but his wife had already died of her injuries. I remember how Johan smiled as that man begged for his life while Johan practiced tightening the knots of wire. That man was his first kill.

"After that, he resisted me less and less. I made certain to take him where he could hear the women scream as vicious men beat them. It kept his mother's torture uppermost in his mind. We used these men to practice on before we killed them."

"How did you kill them?"

"We cut off the heads, Lady, as taught to us by the scar-faced vampire. That was how he killed his own kind before he left us there to die."

Rhonda was clenching and unclenching her hands, but Igor took her gently by the shoulders. "Stay focused now, my pretty bird. Keep your eye on the prize."

She nodded then stepped away from him. "Melosh, go back to the boy before his first kill. What was he like? What joy did he find in life?"

"Little or none, Lady, except the stars at night. He would stare at them for hours. I would try to bring his mind back to the holy quest, but he told me we had become the monsters, every bit as evil as the creatures we sought to find and kill. At times he told me he would finish the quest, then end his own life to rejoin his mother. He said monsters of any kind don't belong in this world, once the vampires are dead there will be no place for us here."

"He never had a girlfriend?"

"No lady, no women for Johan, except the ghost of his mother. The only way a woman could draw his attention would be to scream in pain, then he would run to the rescue. No, he said we were monsters, and no woman should ever have to love a monster."

"Did you get all that recorded, Nikka?"

"Yes, Lady Hawk."

"Good. Igor, take Melosh back to his cell, please. Nikka, fetch Justine for me, would you?"

"At once, Highness."

Rhonda gave her a stern look and pointed at the door. Giggling, she fled. Rhonda smiled as the girl vanished from the room. "Thanks, Nikka, I needed that bit of mischief."

Victor had just walked in and he chuckled at that as Rhonda began to relax. Nikka soon returned with Justine. "Hey, Ronni, what's up?"

"Justine, you minored in psychology, didn't you?"

"Yeah, so?"

"I want you to listen to an interview and tell me what you think." She nodded at Nikka who started the playback.

Justine sat quietly, listening to the interview. "That's one sick and sorry individual." She sighed as the tape finished.

"Can't argue that, but it's not him I'm interested in, it's the other one, the boy who became the man/monster."

"Johan."

"Yes."

"What do you want to know?"

"What will he do now, do you think? What'll he do if he knows we're hunting him? If we put the pressure on him, what'll he do, where will he go?"

"Oh, well, I imagine that, if you push him hard, he'll go back to where his mother was killed."

"Expecting to die there."

"That would be my guess, yes. Ronni, there's not a lot to go on here, and I'm no Amanda or Clyde. Maybe you should send this to them, get their feedback."

"As I remember, you were always good at animal psychology. Nikka, send that off to Amanda with a request for feedback on Johan, please. I bet she comes to the same conclusion you did, J. Okay, Victor, can you go to Melosh and get us the coordinates for that village where they were attacked?"

"On it, Highness." He grinned as he bowed and left the room.

Rhonda made a face at him and he grinned even broader as he left. He returned shortly with the location of the village written on a piece of paper. He passed it to her with a smile. Her phone buzzed, and she glanced down at it. "Gudrun's in the air. It'll be later tonight before they arrive. Where's Peter?"

"He's gone to the village for supplies, Lady," said Victor. "Peter has connection in St. Petersburg who can do some preliminary work for us."

"That's awesome. Dammit, I should have thought of that. Victor, are there other things I've overlooked?"

"Just a few."

"Like what?"

"Lady we, the vampires, all have some form of network, or resources available to us, things we have developed over the years."

"Okay, and?"

"When Peter returns he will have new identification for all of you, passports stamped and everything in order. You know, just in case."

"Dammit, I should have thought of that."

"No, Lady, you're focused on the main mission. We're your supporters, it's our task to take care of the small details. I had this in motion before you arrived. All will be ready when you need it."

"You had it in motion? Talk to me, Victor."

"Lady Hawk, you're focused on the task of keeping this madman from exposing us to the rest of the world. I'm a detail man, I take care of the small things. When we heard you were in charge, and on your way, I started the process just in case. Everything was ready, but Peter was planning a trip to the village today anyway, so he's picking up the items for us."

"So, you're like Gudrun's Eric, the procurer?"

"Yes, like Eric. I find the things you need, and if I can't find them, I invent them. Lady Hawk, you stay focused on the main mission, leave the details to me."

"I'm happy to do just that, but I have to say, you seem to be enjoying your job more than one might expect. What aren't you telling me?"

His smile broadened as he nodded. "Yes, Highness, I am enjoying this. Centuries ago, before I was made vampire, I was in the service of another princess. I was quite happy with my life then, especially serving the young lady. Sadly, war came, and she was killed trying to escape the area. Peter found me and changed me so I could avenge the princess.

"Lady Hawk, I was born into royal service, and I enjoy being useful, especially to someone who appreciates my efforts. Oddly, it gives me a sense of place, of belonging. I actually find it comforting."

"You're serious."

"I am, Highness."

"Then I thank you for your service, and promise to call on you often, my friend. Tell me, are you aware of Queen Sally's visions?"

"Only in that Peter says the king has been guided by them to raise you to the status of his heir."

"In her visions, Victor, I become the queen with three close companions and advisors, Gudrun, Ella, and you."

"Me?"

"Yes, I'm thinking you'll become my main go-to guy for all the stuff I forget."

He laughed with delight at that. "It will be an honor to serve, Highness. Shall I go await Peter's return?"

She nodded so he bowed slightly then left the room. "Igor?"

"Yes, my pretty bird?"

"When this is all over, remind me to spend some time getting to know more about all the vampires as well as the wolves."

"I will, sweet Ronni," he smiled. "I will."

Hunted

It had been a long and exhausting drive, but Johan was finally approaching Moscow. He'd called ahead to warn the men to be on full alert but hadn't liked the tone of the man he'd spoken with. Obviously, they'd been talking to some of the deserters from St. Petersburg. He'd have to do some convincing to get them back onside.

With a sudden jerk, he came fully alert again, narrowly missing an oncoming truck. As the angry sound of its horn faded behind him, Johan looked for a place to pull over and sleep. He was exhausted. He pulled off the road and shut off the motor. Tipping the seat back, he sighed and closed his eyes.

"It won't be long now, Mother. Soon I will join you among the stars, but first I have some vampires to kill. At least I'm finally free of Melosh. Better still, the vampires will probably hunt me now, much easier to find them that way."

He slept fitfully, the nightmares of his past deeds haunting him. Melosh would never accept the truth, but Johan knew, they had become the monsters, every bit as evil as the ones they hunted. Johan awakened in a cold sweat, an unreasoning fear crawling up his spine. He shook it off and looked for someplace to relieve himself. It was dark now, and once back in the car he drove more carefully as he approached the outskirts of the city.

WHILE JOHAN CAUTIOUSLY approached Moscow, a stealth plane swept across the Russia / Finland border, barely above the treetops. In mere moments it settled to the ground in the compound where Peter and Rhonda stood waiting.

The crew threw the tarp over the plane while Rhonda hugged Gudrun. Gudrun stepped back, grinning. "See, little sister, I'm good as new."

"Awesome. Let's get this show on the road. Come inside. We'll bring you up to speed then you can take over."

"Sorry, but no."

"Excuse me?"

"Honey, this is your command. I'll do everything I can to help you, but you're in charge."

Rhonda went nose to nose with the grinning vampire. "Listen you, I put up with this stuff from the rest, but you promised to keep me grounded. Stop acting the fool and take charge."

Gudrun kissed the tip of her nose and grinned harder. "Nope."

Rhonda stared at her for several moments, then she got it. "You're trying to teach me something, aren't you?"

That smile brightened. "Yes, my sister, I am. Think like a commander now."

Again Lady Hawk brooded for several moments. Finally she sighed and allowed her shoulders to relax. "Okay, my mission, I have a job to do, and several assets to help me get it done. Gudrun, you're the most experienced at this sort of action. Let's all go inside, we'll bring you up to speed, then you can advise me as to what we should do next." With that she turned and marched back inside.

The others followed closely, and Peter guided her to a different room. This one was much larger and resembled Harald's great hall. He indicated Rhonda should take the head of table seat then the others sat.

"All right, people," she began, "we have a major problem here. We've discovered a network of vampire hunters that threatens to expose us to the world at large. We need to stop that from happening and we need to move on it quickly.

"In our favor, we have a full list of the network members, their addresses, and the locations of their training centers. We know the methods they use to capture and confine their victims, and we know they've recorded the methods many time as they practiced on human captives.

"Working against us: Their leader has evaded us for the moment, and we do need to capture him. He's the only living member of the network still at large who has actually seen a real vampire. The other is held captive in this facility.

"Issues that hinder us: I'm the person in command here, but the network we seek to destroy is in Europe, and I only speak English, plus, I have no experience in this sort of operation.

"How I'd like to proceed: This network was built, trained, and maintained by two men, we have one in captivity, the other remains at large. They recorded their crimes, and we have that evidence. It's my thought to capture the other leader, then distribute the evidence to various police forces, let them take down this network of serial killers for us.

"We also have video evidence of Gudrun's torture; however, on that video there is no evidence of a vampire, just a woman being tortured. I'd like to capture a few of those men, take them and the two leaders back to the scene of the crime, then have Gudrun's crew stage a rescue of their commander. The police will see a band of mercenaries rescue their leader, and no other evidence at all.

"Gudrun, you are now my second-in-command, you have the most experience here, advise me. Is this feasible and, if so, what's our next move?"

Gudrun rose and smiled at Rhonda with true delight. "Yes, Highness, I believe your plan is quite feasible, and I like it. I agree, tracking down and capturing the other leader should be our first priority, however, we need to be aware of his network. He could be raising a small army right now, expecting us to come after him.

"Do we know where he would be likely to go?"

"We do. Our captive believes he would go to the training center in St. Petersburg, with Moscow as the second most likely retreat. We can assume he'll be expecting us to come at him, so he might try evasion. Our resident shrink believes that, if we push him hard enough he'll probably return to the village where Mobutu slaughtered his family. We have a location for that place as well.

"Now, you folks have had a long flight, and you need to rest. Nikka, give Ella and Gudrun all the evidence we've gathered."

"At once, Lady Hawk." Nikka rose and hurried out of the room.

"Okay, folks, study what we have, you can question Melosh if you wish, then once you've had a chance to rest, we'll meet back here and come up with a plan of action. Right now, I'm going out and sleep under the stars with a pack of wolves to keep me warm."

With that Rhonda strode from the room with Igor at her side. Nikka came back in, laid the materials on the table then hurried after them. Gudrun was shaking her head and grinning. "Well, Mother, what do you think?"

Ella chuckled at that. "I think you've just created a monarch. She does have a good grasp on the situation, though, and I like her plan for dealing with this mess."

"So do I. In fact, it improves on what I had in mind. Ronni's right, why should we shut down the whole network if we can get the human police to do it for us. What do you think, Terry?"

"Yeah, I like it. The hard part will be tracking down and acquiring the target. Once we have him the rest is a piece of cake."

"All right then, let's look over what we've got here and see if we can find a way to make that easier. I want to look good in the eyes of the new heir." Ella chuckled at that and opened the file.

Wolf Queen

Rhonda slowly opened her eyes but didn't stir. She was naked, cuddled between two wolves, Igor and Nikka. The rest of the pack was close by. "Okay, Ronni, you know what you have to do now." She sighed to herself. "Yeah, but I'll damn well want a coffee afterwards."

Steeling her resolve she sat up and beamed her brightest smile at Igor and the wolves. As soon as she moved, they were awake, looking to her. She ruffled Igor's fur then stood and stretched. The wolves arose and shook themselves, then stood waiting.

"Thank you, my beautiful wolves, my friends, for guarding my sleep and keeping me warm. Now, let's hunt up some breakfast." With a piercing cry, she leaped into the air and climbed skyward. She was soon making a wide lazy circle to the right, the alpha wolf below keeping a close eye on her.

Her circle changed to a tight circle to the left and the wolves set out. Below the circling hawk they found an old bull elk and soon brought him down. The beast was dead and the wolves backed away as the hawk plummeted to the ground and began ripping at the meat.

She ate her fill then flew up to circle overhead, watching for danger while first the alpha fed then the rest of the pack. When all had eaten she flew off toward the compound, the wolves running easily below her. Suddenly her sharp eyes caught movement. She called a warning then circled tightly to the right.

At that signal Igor went on full alert. The pack seemed to melt into the trees and vanish. Slowly, two men with guns, hunters, moved quietly into the small clearing, eyes darting. One man spotted a wolf and raised his rifle.

The hawk called another warning then dropped from the sky like a stone. The hunter screamed as razor sharp talon raked at his face and wings buffeted him. His friend batted the hawk away, but it transformed into a naked woman and struck. A small fist, driven by the strength of an immortal, cracked against his jaw and he melted to the ground, unconscious.

The first man had cleared his vision, but the hawk was already in the air once again. What he now saw was a powerfully built man surrounded by a pack of wolves. "There is no hunting allowed in this forest."

"I can hunt wherever I wish," he snarled in reply.

"Take your friend and leave this place, never return. If you do, the people of the forest will kill you. You've been warned. Go now."

The second man was reviving, and his friend helped him to stand. Reluctantly they took their rifles and started away, but the hawk dropped to the ground and transformed. She was angry and letting it show. With a single step she reached them and jerked the weapons from their hands. Rhonda smashed the rifles against a tree then leaped back into the sky.

The two hunters were dumbfounded. They looked up at the hawk in the sky then turned to Igor. "The goddess of the forest is angry with you for trespassing on her hunting ground. Leave now and do not return. Next time she may command me to kill you."

He watched them until they disappeared from sight, then he transformed, looked up at the hawk, then led the pack as they followed her back to the compound. She dropped down into the middle of the pack and transformed. "All right, family, this girl needs coffee, who's with me?"

Grinning, Igor took her arm. "Should we find some clothes first?"

Her silvery laughter floated across the brisk morning air, a song of pure joy. "Yes, my lover, let's find some clothes."

"Right here, Lady Hawk." Lidiya smiled, as she appeared with a cart loaded with long tunics, soft leather shoes, and woolen robes.

They swiftly dressed and headed for the dining hall. Rhonda linked her arm through Igor's then the other arm through Illya's. They escorted her to the table and Lidiya set a huge mug of coffee at her right hand.

As the mug appeared, Rhonda tasted it, and it was mixed exactly the way she liked it. She looked up to thank the girl and smiled. "Is it to your liking, Highness?"

"It's perfect, Lidiya, thank you. How did you know how I like my coffee?"

The girl grinned as she replied. "I cheated, Highness. I called Elaine at the Lair and asked her what I needed to do for you. This was the first thing she told me."

Rhonda laughed with delight. "A resourceful woman, I like that. So, are you a werewolf, or something else?"

"Alas, Lady, I'm just a lowly human."

The lady hawk reached out and took the girl by the hand. "Lidiya, there is nothing lowly about being human, nothing. You're as necessary to us as any other. The idea here is to find a way to keep my people alive and safe, but also to find ways for us all to live in harmony together. Humans are as important to us as any other. Besides, you brought me coffee, you're invaluable to me." She gently squeezed the girl's hand then released her.

Lidiya lowered her eyes and blushed. "Thank you, Highness. Lady, may I ask a favor?"

Rhonda's eyes snapped back to her. "Sure. How can I help?"

"Lady, a certain werewolf and I want to marry. He had worked up his courage to approach the alpha, but then there came a new alpha, and then a queen ..."

Rhonda was grinning, mischief dancing in her eyes. "This wolf of yours, a bit shy, is he?"

"He's not highly placed in the pack, Lady, but he is a gentle man, and I love him."

"Well, that decision belongs to the alpha, but I'll put in a good word for you. Igor?"

"Da, permission granted." He, too, was wearing a grin of delight.

"Bring him to me, Lidiya," smiled Rhonda. Wide-eyed she hurried away and soon returned dragging a young man behind her. "So, are you sure about this, Lidiya? The wolf mates for life, do this and you're stuck with him forever."

"That's the plan, Lady."

"Very well then. What's your name, my fine young wolf?"

"I am Arvad, Queen Lady Hawk."

"So, do you swear to cherish and protect Lidiya and all the children she brings to you from this moment forward?"

"I do, my queen."

"Lidiya, do you swear to love and cherish Arvad, and do you fully understand any children you bear him will belong to the pack, that you will become part of the pack?"

"I do, and I understand, Lady."

"Igor, as grand alpha of all the wolves, do you approve this union?"

He was grinning and winked at Arvad. They had been in the death camp together. "Da, Queen Lady Hawk. I approve."

"Done then. I now pronounce you wolf and wife."

Lidiya had tears in her eyes. In truth, all she'd dare to hope for was permission. "Highness, I ..."

"Go on, get out of here and go play. Let me finish my coffee." The girl matched Rhonda's grin then grabbed her new husband by the hand and dragged him out of the room.

Rhonda resumed her seat to see Illya smiling at her. "What?"

"I have badly misjudged you, my queen. I'm sorry for that."

"We didn't have time to get better acquainted, Illya. Things happened quickly for Igor and me, and then you were gone. You've always done your best for your people, and I swear to do the same."

"I believe you, and I am now at peace with the way things have worked out." She reached over and gave his hand a gentle squeeze.

Another coffee mug hit the table and Gudrun sat across from Rhonda. "Looks like you've had a busy morning."

"I have."

"That was sweet, what you did there."

"He's one of mine, I need to help him if I can. Besides, I like the girl."

"And?"

"And I needed that as badly as they did. I needed a spoonful of happy before going to war again. Did you get a chance to interview Melosh?"

"Yes."

"Is he still alive?"

"For now."

Ella joined them. She smiled as she passed Rhonda a fresh mug of coffee. "So, Ronni, I hear you officiate at weddings now. Don't you need some sort of certificate for that?"

"Hey, I'm queen of the werewolves, who better to tie the knot for them?"

"I think you like the new status."

"Tease if you must, Ella; however, I like my wolf people, a lot, and I'll do my best for them."

"But?"

They were both grinning now. "They're a bunch of savages, Ella. They made me sleep outdoors, and made me eat raw meat, and ..."

Ella laughed and reached to gently squeeze Igor's shoulder. "So, your wild hawk went full wolf for you, did she?"

"Da," he grinned. "She's wilder than ever now. Great Mother, what am I to do?"

"Hang on for the ride, little brother," grinned Gudrun.

They were still chuckling when Rhonda suddenly looked up. "What is it?" asked Igor.

"I see Terry, but not Kylie. Ella, didn't she come with you?"

"No, Harald didn't send her, should he have?"

"Men," muttered Rhonda. "I'll have a chat with the king. You need to have her with you at all times. From now on, any mission I lead with you on the team will also have Kylie."

"Ronni?"

"Your time together is finite, Ella, you should not have been parted. We need to wrap this up and get you home."

Gudrun's eyes went hard as she rose from the table. "Then let's get to work."

On the Hunt

They returned to the war room, as Rhonda had taken to calling the large meeting room. "All right, folks, let's get to it. Gudrun, you've got a network of people all over Europe, yes?"

"I do, Ronni."

"Anybody in St. Petersburg?"

"I don't believe so, I ..."

"We don't need them there," said Nikka, as she entered the room. "Sorry, Miss Gudrun. We've just heard a newscast. The place in St. Petersburg has been found by the police, empty except for several dead bodies. The authorities are searching for a serial killer who ties up his victims with razor wire, tortures them, then leaves them to die."

The room had gone silent. Rhonda shook it off and spoke first. "Well, crap. Thank you, Nikka. Okay then, according to Melosh, Moscow would be his next stop. Got anybody there, Gudrun?"

"I do," said Terry. "At least, I used to."

"So do I," grinned Gudrun.

"All right then, you guys see what news you can gather from there. If Moscow is a go, what's our fastest way there?"

"The plane," said Eric. "We'll go make sure she's well stocked up. Let's go guys." He led the other soldiers out. Terry was on his phone to someone, and so was Gudrun. He was speaking English, and she was speaking in Russian. Rhonda sighed and sat back in her chair. She hated waiting, unable to take any action.

Terry sighed and dropped his phone back into his pocket. "I got nothing about Moscow, but we're clear on St. Petersburg. All the cops found there was two dead men, shot, who were wanted for murder, and two more corpses wrapped up in wire. They'd been tortured then left to die. Both of those men were identified as being wanted for murder also.

"Now there's a nationwide manhunt for a killer who targets violent criminals and tortures them to death. I'd say we're clear from there and can go straight to Moscow. Obviously, our bird has flown from St. Petersburg."

"I agree," said Gudrun. "My people in Moscow have nothing useful for us. I've asked them to keep watch on the training facility there but didn't tell them what it was. I also have them watching for our man. I gave them a full description, told them not to engage, but to locate and mark him for me. We should move out."

"I agree, let's go," said Rhonda, grateful for some action, any action. "Peter, thank you for all you've done for us, and for the stellar hospitality. If we don't come back this way, I promise to come for a visit often. Do you want to accompany us to Moscow?"

"Thank you, Highness, but I'll remain here. This sanctuary is always open to you, and you are always welcome here. I'll fetch Melosh for you now. We'll meet you outside by the plane."

They were already aboard the plane when Melosh joined them. Still fully under the compulsion to obey Rhonda, he sat watching her, waiting for her to give him direction. The plane rose easily into the air and moved swiftly away to the east.

"Melosh, when we arrive in Moscow, keep your eye out for Johan. If you see him, tell me instantly, but don't try to speak to him or catch his attention."

"I understand, Lady Hawk. I will do as you command."

"Good boy, lower your eyes to your hands now until we arrive."

"Yes, ma'am," he replied, as he folded his hands in his lap and lowered his gaze.

Igor put his arm around her shoulders. "What's troubling you, my pretty bird?"

"We need to come back here once this is over."

"Oh?"

"You need more time with this pack, and I need to learn Russian."

"Ronni?"

"I need to learn them all, Igor, every language I can. I feel so helpless here, having to work through interpreters."

"You don't trust ..."

"Oh no, sweetie, I trust our people implicitly, I just ..."

"Want to do it all yourself?"

She chuckled at that. "Yeah, that. No, it's just that I feel helpless. What will I do if we get separated, how can I ask questions, find food or shelter, locate my own people, care for them, make sure they're happy and secure ..."

"Okay, I get it, sweet Ronni. When we get back Miss Gudrun can teach you Russian, Marlene can teach you French, the king can teach German, and I'm sure Miss Ella knows a few others. We will help you, my love, but first we make an end of these vampire hunters, then the goddess of the forest can go to school."

His last remark caught the attention of Ella and Gudrun. Grinning, he told of how Rhonda had seen the danger to the wolves, saved them from it, then confronted the hunters and destroyed their weapons.

"Rhonda, you showed yourself?"

"It's all right, Ella. Those men saw a hawk who became a woman who became a hawk who became a woman, a small woman who knocked out a large man with a single punch, and then snatched away their toys and broke them. They also saw a naked man commanding a pack of gigantic wolves. Now, who are these big strong men going to tell this story to?"

"No, they'll drown their sorrows in vodka and convince themselves they'd gotten some bad drugs or something, they'll never tell anyone else a naked woman half their size broke their toys and sent them home."

"Still, it would have been much better if someone there could have used the compulsion on them."

"I agree, but alas, that's one talent that didn't come with the immortal t-shirt. I have to depend on the male ego. You're right, what I did was rash and foolish. What should I have done?"

"You should have stopped them, which you did, then the wolves should have killed them," said Gudrun. "My sister, you're still protecting the lives of your enemies. You have to get past that."

"I thought I had. These men weren't the enemy, they were just hunters in the wrong place."

"Easy, my sister, easy. I'm not criticizing you; I'm trying to help you."

"Gudrun, these men weren't the enemy. I can't just kill them for no reason."

Gudrun sighed and reached for Rhonda, taking her from Igor's arms and hugging her gently. "Tell me exactly what happened."

"I saw the hunters, one was aiming his rifle at the wolves. I dropped down and attacked him, but his partner batted me to the ground. I transformed and decked him, then leaped back into the air. Igor transformed and spoke to them, told them the goddess of the forest was angry with them. It looked like one of them was going to try again so I landed, took their guns away and smashed them."

"Okay, now, take a deep breath, queen of the wolves, and tell me again. What happened?"

Puzzled, Rhonda moved back to gaze into her eyes. Slowly the light of understanding reached her, and she sighed, let her shoulders slump, and melted back into Gudrun's arms. "I saw two hunters aim weapons at my people. I stopped them, but I let them go. In the future they'll probably hunt and kill wolves again, maybe even one of mine, exposing us to the world. I blew it, unnecessarily risked my people, exposed the existence of non-humans, and hung it all on fragile human egos."

"And the lesson is?"

"They're not my species anymore, they're predators, dangerous, and need to be treated as such. Dammit, I fucked up big time. I'm so not the right one to be doing this. I'll get everybody killed. Stop playing around and take command here, Gudrun, for everybody's sake."

"Nope. You're queen of the wolves, heir to the throne of the non-humans, your job, not mine."

"Can't I abdicate?"

"Nope, not allowed."

"Says who?" demanded Rhonda, a grin touching her lips in spite of herself.

"We do," smiled Ella. "This is your cross to bear, but mother and big sister are here to help." Rhonda looked puzzled so Ella chuckled and went on. "Ronni, from now on, when you run with the wolves, I will be there too. My compulsion is the strongest.

"Besides, for over a million years I was a solitary hunter, but that's not my true nature. Saber-toothed tigers were group hunters, much like modern day lions. It'll be good to run with a pack, and I'll be there to help you.

"Ronni, since I bullied Harald into being king, I've found a life I love as part of this odd little monarchy. Harald will make you his heir, and I've sworn to him that I'll serve you as loyally as I do him, and I meant that. I've found my place, and now I want to help you find yours."

"The same goes for me," smiled Gudrun, as she gently passed Rhonda back to Igor's arms. "Lady Hawk, I'll serve you as loyally as I do the king. More, you know what happened back there when you rescued me. You know we're truly sisters now. Ronni, we'll do whatever needs to be done to help and support you."

"You're going to make me do this, aren't you, all of you. Why?"

"Because you're a born leader," said Igor. "It's true, sweet Ronni. It scares you, but it's true. When shit hits the fan sideways, you always take over and make things happen. Look how you got Miss Gudrun back. You can see what must be done, then you do it. Now you have to see a bigger picture, but you have help. The great mother is here, the super soldier, and the alpha, we are here to help, advise, and guide, as you need."

"Ronni, when I was learning to lead soldiers, I made mistakes, plenty of them. It took me a lot of years to hone my skills. This experience is available to you now, to help you adjust to the new job. Don't beat yourself up, girl, just let us help you."

"This is so weird," sighed Rhonda. "All my life I've had to rely on myself. It was always up to me to get things done for others, but I was left on my own to do it."

"Having trouble accepting help?" asked Ella.

"Yeah, I guess, maybe an old trust issue or two there as well."

Gudrun smiled. "Come on, sis, give us a chance to prove our trust. Know this, we will never knowingly do anything to harm or endanger you or your wolves. The non-humans as well as our human allies are your people now also; they're ours too. We'll work together to protect them, with you leading us. Okay?"

"Deal," chuckled Rhonda. "We can start now. Ella, you're up."

"What? I don't understand."

"Ella, a number of times I've endangered my people, and probably put them in the way of possible exposure. Igor said it best long ago, someone in my past convinced me that men were more important than anything else, and if possible, they should never be harmed, especially killed.

"When I have the time to reason things out, I have no problems, but in the heat of the moment I make mistakes, react on instinct, old conditioning. I need you to use that powerful compulsion on me, get me past that conditioning. I can't afford to put my people in danger unnecessarily."

Ella slowly nodded. "And by allowing me to use the compulsion on you, you demonstrate trust. I understand, Highness. So be it.

"Rhonda, you are queen of the werewolves. They are your people, we non-humans are your people, we are your subjects. You will never again

take unnecessary chances with the lives of your subjects. You will no longer put the welfare of a human above the welfare of your own people. You are the queen, accept that, and trust that we want it this way. It is our desire for you to be so."

"There now, that should do it."

"Ella, thanks for that."

"Ronni, you didn't need that, you just need a bit of adjustment time."

"That may be so, Ella, but we don't have that kind of time right now. For now, I'm more than happy to have your help."

The plane landed and taxied into a hangar, well hidden from the public eye. They got out and Gudrun led them to an office. A woman was waiting there. She spoke to Gudrun and pointed to a door. Gudrun thanked her then led the women into a large changing room. Clothing had been laid out for them, and they swiftly dressed. Rhonda smiled at the warmth of the wool dress and the fur coat.

"I made a few arrangements in case we came this way," grinned Gudrun. "Come, ladies, the boys will be waiting."

They returned to the office and the woman pointed to the door. Outside the office, Eric and the others were waiting in a mini bus. An hour later they were on the opposite side of the city, driving slowly along by the warehouses. Eric stopped to let a destitute woman get aboard.

Once in the bus, she shed the disguise and grinned, addressing Gudrun. "In English, Merilla."

"Of course," she replied, puzzled. "Since when do you bring a client on a mission?"

"Look closer."

The woman's eyes snapped back to Ella and then to Rhonda. She swallowed hard then returned her attention to Gudrun. "I found the secret entrance to the building, Gudrun. It's good you have a full team for these people. These are dangerous and nasty men."

"But?"

"These scum aren't your usual kind of target. I wonder who would pay you to go after men like these."

"This is personal," said Rhonda, as she gripped the woman's shoulder hard enough to break bone. "I want their leader, a man named Johan. He tortured my sister; for this he will pay with his life, for I'll hunt him to the ends of the earth if I have to. This man will die by her hand."

Wide-eyed and amazed at the power of her grip, the woman swallowed hard. "Yes, ma'am. The man Gudrun described to me entered the building late last night. As far as I know, he's still in there."

"Gudrun, take command, get this done."

"At once, Highness. Eric, there."

The sun was just going down, and the long shadows hid their movements. Eric parked the van and Vassily leaped out to hurl himself against the door. It didn't give so he slapped something on it and turned away. A heartbeat later, the door exploded inward. Jimmy, Terry, and Eric leaped inside, followed by Vassily and Gudrun. The place looked empty.

Gudrun signaled and Rhonda followed her in, flanked by Ella and Igor. Melosh, looking terrified, followed. "Melosh, where?"

"There, Lady, that way. There's a trapdoor near the back wall. Everything is below this level."

"Show us."

He led the way then stepped back as Eric lifted the door. It triggered an alarm and a hail of gunfire came through, but he'd stepped back and was unharmed. Vassily tossed a flash grenade down the hole, then Gudrun and her soldiers followed it down. There were several disoriented men there, trying to clear their vision. They were immediately put in restraints.

"Lady Hawk, Lady Hawk ..."

"What is it?"

"I saw Johan, Lady Hawk. You said to ..."

"Where?"

"That way, Lady. He went out through the escape tunnel through the sewers." They rushed toward the doorway at the far end of area, but it exploded, driving them back. He'd escaped them again. Cursing madly, Gudrun led her troops back up the stairs and outside.

"Melosh, what will they find?"

"It is too late now, Lady. Johan has escaped."

"Where will he go?"

"I don't know. Perhaps Helsinki, but I doubt that, not Warsaw either."

"Why not?"

"He saw me, Lady. He knows now."

"Merilla."

"Yes?" The note of command in Rhonda's voice caught her attention. She had heard Gudrun call this one Highness, and knew she was to be obeyed. Worse, the more silent woman and the young man exuded a danger she did not want to antagonize.

"You see these men encased in wire?" The torture victims were moaning, begging with their eyes for release, for help.

"Yes. Shall I find some way to cut the wire?"

"No. Wait until we've gone, then call the authorities and inform them of what they'll find here. Make no mention of me or my people."

"As you desire." She said nothing more, but the question was clear in her eyes.

"She is the Lady Hawk," said Igor, as he stepped closer. "She is to be obeyed in all things. Ask nothing more." Merilla nodded but didn't speak. This woman had some extremely dangerous companions, and they were obviously devoted to her, so was Gudrun. Merilla wanted nothing to do with the idea of pissing her off.

"Ella."

"Yes, Highness?"

"These men are not to remember our visit. Speak to them and instruct them to await the police."

"As you command, Highness," grinned Ella. Rhonda rolled her eyes, then led Igor and the others back up the stairs and out to the waiting van. Ella soon joined them.

Gudrun and troops returned empty-handed. She was swearing in three languages and Terry was trying to calm her. "The scum escaped us. He had these men organized and prepared to fight us. Notice they were using tranquilizer loads and not live ammo. He'll probably head for the next likely group."

"Melosh, will he go to Finland, do you think?"

"No, Lady Hawk. I know him well. Johan will know I'm with you because he saw me. Now he believes you will go to the facility in Helsinki, so he will go to Hamburg, or perhaps Warsaw. If you defeat him there he will double back to Helsinki."

"Gudrun?"

"We need to get there first, be waiting for him. Mount up. Merilla."

"I have my instructions, Gudrun. I'll take care of this."

Gudrun turned to Rhonda who winked and gave a quick jerk of her head. With a grin Merilla couldn't see, Gudrun got into the van. "Yes, ma'am." The van drove away, leaving Merilla behind.

"Igor, is she always this bossy?"

"You have no idea," he replied, with an elaborate sigh.

"Shut up, both of you," giggled Rhonda, as she poked him in the ribs.

As they rode back to the plane, Gudrun was busy on the phone. Finally she settled back and sighed. "All right, we have people on the lookout for him. Melosh, what's your best guess, Hamburg or Warsaw?"

He didn't respond, nor give any indication she had spoken. "Answer her."

"Yes, Lady Hawk. Warsaw is closer, so he will be more likely to go to Hamburg. Defeat him there and he will retreat to Helsinki, then to Warsaw. This is only a guess, but I have seen his book, some of the plans and defensive strategies he's worked on over the years."

"He's worked on retreat plans?"

"We both did, Lady Hawk. We always knew the vampire might discover us hunting him, that we might become the hunted instead of the hunters. The plan was to fall back to a stronghold, hide behind the traps, and capture the beast in that way."

"Speak to me of these traps."

"Answer her, Melosh."

"We planned to retreat through the tunnels, trigger the knockout gas, capture the vampire. We didn't have Moscow fully set up yet. It was to be our next stop after the training exercise in Finland. Hamburg will have such traps, as will Warsaw."

"What about London?"

"He will avoid London, Lady Hawk. He got in trouble there and doesn't dare go back."

"Hamburg it is. I'll hide in the plane while you deal with it, Gudrun."

"You'll hide in the plane? Why, for god's sake?"

"No German ID. Keep a low profile?"

"It's on the plane, Highness," grinned Eric as he stopped the van at the hangar where they'd left the plane. "Victor gave it to me as we were prepping for takeoff. You're good to go in Germany, Poland, Russia, Finland, France, England, and Sweden."

Rhonda shook her head and grinned as they boarded the plane. "Looks like my details guy is way ahead of me again. The man's amazing."

Ella settled in beside her. "He's been an invaluable resource to us each time we have to establish a new identity. We often turn to Victor for such things."

The Hunt Goes On

Rhonda was gazing at her passport as the plane took off and headed for Hamburg, Germany. It had official looking stamps for every European country they might have to visit. "Remind me to find a way to properly thank him." Ella smiled and patted her hand.

They landed at a hangar owned by one of Gudrun's companies. It was swiftly inside, out of sight of prying eyes. A man met them as they disembarked and spoke to Gudrun. "In English please, Albert." He gave her a quirked eyebrow, but switched easily, taking note of how Gudrun stepped back slightly to allow Rhonda front and center.

"All our people are in place, Gudrun. The building has been marked and watched. The men on your list are all there and they are armed. Our listening devices tell us they are preparing for an attack by vampires. We also hear screams of torment. What madness is this?"

It was Lady Hawk who answered him. "Just that. Madness. Their leader is on his way here, or so we believe. He's the one we want alive."

The man turned and stepped closer to Rhonda as she spoke. "Oh, and why is that?"

Gudrun was instantly between them, nose to nose with the man. "That's the lady's business, and not yours. You have two tasks, focus on those and nothing more. One, find this man for us, two, never speak of this to anyone."

He swallowed hard and stepped back. "Of course, Gudrun."

He stepped back and turned away, cursing himself for that stupid remark. He stepped through the door and pulled out his phone. Suddenly the silent woman was beside him. "Who are you calling."

"That is not your business."

To his great shock she grabbed him and hurled him back through the door. "*Who were you calling?*"

Trembling with fear he replied in spite of himself. "The chief of the police."

"Why?"

"He pays me to inform him of anything interesting concerning Gudrun's activities."

"You will wait until we leave the city to make your report. When we have gone you will report that Gudrun and her people did nothing of interest while they were here. You are utterly devoted to Gudrun and will protect her at all cost. Go now."

"I understand." With that, he turned and walked away.

Rhonda watched him go then sighed. "So now what?"

"Now we wait, my sister. We're a few days ahead of Johan, so we settle down to wait. There's a safe house nearby that we own. We'll settle in there and wait. Relax, Highness, this time we'll let the prey come to us."

JOHAN DROVE WEST, RARELY stopping. He passed through Belarus and into Poland, bypassed Warsaw and headed for the German border. They would be ready by the time he arrived, and he would lead the vampires right to them. He almost smiled as he thought of the vampires and Melosh waiting for him in Warsaw.

Melosh was such a fool, he had never truly understood tactics. The vampires had him now and he would have them waiting for him at Warsaw, but he would not go there, he would go to Hamburg. When the vampires got tired of waiting in Poland, they would move on to the next facility, but he would be there first, waiting to visit their doom upon them.

Nearly falling asleep at the wheel, he stopped at a roadside lookout and tipped the seat back so he could see the stars. To his exhausted mind, the vision of his mother and younger sister came easily. He went to sleep with a promise to join them on his lips. He awakened hours later, screaming, the sounds of Mobutu's laughter ringing in his ears.

Gasping for breath, Johan shook off the nightmare and sat back up. Munching on some junk food, he drove on. After crossing over into Germany, he took a room for the day. He wanted a shower, and he wanted to check in with his people in Hamburg. Everything was ready, and Johan was warned to make contact as he arrived. Someone would have to lead him through the traps.

Feeling much better after a shower, shave, and long nap, Johan smiled as he paid for the room with his credit card. He felt sure that, by now, the vampires had given up in Warsaw and would find his trail by tracking the card. He had no idea at all they were already in Hamburg, anxiously awaiting his arrival.

Johan parked his car and walked over to speak with the man awaiting him. Just as they shook hands, disaster struck. A van screeched to a stop and several people in uniform leaped out. Johan pushed the other man through the door and followed him in, slamming the door behind them. He'd seen her, leading them.

Together they ran down the corridor, dodging the traps as the door they'd closed was blown in. The nets fell and the gas filled the passageway, but it had little effect. These soldiers were carrying sharp knives and wearing gas masks. The weapons had no effect on them either as they were wearing body armor.

Door after door they locked behind them and door after door was blown open. They fled on, finally reaching the rest of the men in the basement, hunkered behind a barricade and heavily armed. Those men screamed in terror at the speed, as two of the attackers leaped the barricade and landed in their midst. Their speed and strength were terrifying. Bodies went flying and men screamed in pain and fear as the rest of the soldiers joined the fray.

Horrified, Johan didn't stop to engage in the fight, he just fled out the back through the escape tunnel. He burst from the manhole right beside his car, but this time he wasn't so lucky. Before he could get the car open a hawk dropped from the sky and raked at his face. With a bellow of surprise and rage he batted the bird aside then leaped into the car and started the engine.

The hawk was already in the air and diving again as he tried to drive away. He gunned the engine and the tires screamed in protest at the sudden acceleration. The diving bird slammed into the windshield, causing him to swerve into another parked car, but not enough to get him stopped. As the slightly stunned bird picked herself up and shook off the cobwebs, his car disappeared around the building.

A soldier ran across the parking lot and scooped up the hawk, then disappeared inside their van. "Are you okay, sweet Ronni?"

"Yeah, I'm fine. Bastard got in a lucky punch. Dammit all to hell, Igor, I nearly had him. Slippery bastard got away on me."

Igor sighed and settled down beside her. "Remind you of anybody?"

"Yes, that little vampire out Oregon way."

"And just like her, we will catch this one and make an end of him."

Eric reappeared and slid behind the wheel as the others returned. Spotting Rhonda, Gudrun dropped to one knee at her feet, reaching for her. "Ronni, what happened?"

"There was no one around so I went up to see if he tried to sneak away again. I saw the rat come out of the sewers and bloodied his nose for him, but I wasn't able to prevent him from reaching his car. Bastard's probably halfway to Warsaw by now at the speed he was going."

"Are you all right?"

"I'll have a few bruises, but nothing to fret about. How about you?"

"Go, Eric. I'm fine, Highness. We defeated their traps with only a few scratches and bruises, captured the men, and searched for Johan to no avail. Mother put the compulsion on them, and they'll forget we were ever there."

Gudrun eased herself into the seat beside Terry who cuddled her into his arms. She kissed Terry's cheek then leaned back and sighed. "Eric, to the plane."

"To the plane. Destination Warsaw?"

"Warsaw. He got away from us again, but we've got him on the run. We'll keep eyes on Helsinki as well, but, according to Melosh, Warsaw is our best bet. If we keep the pressure up, it should drive him back to his beginnings and there to meet his fate."

PUSHING THE SPEED AS much as he dared, Johan fled back toward Poland and a safe house they had just inside the Polish border. "Again, it was her. How did she get there ahead of me? Did she fly? Can they do that, or did she travel in a plane? Who knows. Perhaps Melosh was right after all, there was so much more to learn, wrong information to discover.

"If they were known for so long, why is there so much misinformation out there? Of course, they did it themselves once they were discovered. How long have they been here, or are they the older species? Who knows? Who cares. They are pure evil and must be destroyed. Sadly, it appears I'm unlikely to be the one to accomplish this.

"So, it's back to Warsaw, my last hope to defeat her. Should I fail there, I will return home and join mother in the next world. I tire of this: I'm ready to leave the battle to another. I just pray I don't become one of their pawns like Melosh."

Johan continued to ruminate on the problem until he was back in Poland, secure in the safe house. Lying back on the bed, he started again. He called ahead, and Warsaw was ready. He sighed and began to ponder the likelihood of succeeding. It didn't look promising; they already had Melosh, and as a result, full knowledge of where he might go or what he might do. Reluctantly, Johan admitted defeat.

"So now what do I do? Go home and join Mother? Yes, but can I leave this world without any warning, any actual truth about these beasts? Is there a way to dispel all the misinformation and shine some light on the monsters in our midst? Perhaps, but how?

"Go to the police? With what we have done they would simple execute me or lock me in an institution, fill me with drugs, and say I'm completely crazy. Who knows, perhaps that might be the best solution. No, then the information would be lost. No, this journal in my hand is the only real information out there, the vampires will have destroyed Melosh's computer by now.

"I could go to the internet. No, the internet is full of crazy people already. I would be laughed off as a fool and ignored or tormented. Besides, the vampires may already have control of that place. No, I need something more, something different. Yes, something older, safer, a place where I can speak freely, yet remain safe.

"Better yet, an organization that will have a faction that would believe me. Dammit, Melosh, you old fool, that's where we should have gone in the first place to look for help, instead you made me a worse monster than the vampire." With that sudden resolve, Johan rose from the bed and dressed.

It was dark out, but there was enough light in the village for Johan to find his way. A short walk later he found the old church. He tried the door and found it unlocked. The inside was dimly lit with flickering candles. As the door clunked shut behind him, a man in priest's robes came through a side door and approached him.

"The hour is late, my son. Have you come to pray, or to confess your sin?"

"To confess my sins, Father, and they are many. I'm not Catholic; will you still hear me?"

"Of course, my son, the Lord is always ready to hear a heartfelt confession. Right this way."

He led Johan to the confessional and settled him inside. Once he was ready, Johan began. "Forgive me, Father, for I have sinned. I believe this is how the ritual starts."

"Go ahead, my son."

He did. Johan spoke of his life, from the day the vampire attacked the church, up to the moment he'd walked in. He confessed it all, the tortures, the killings, Gudrun's capture, and eventual escape, down to her pursuit of him across Europe.

"They are now closing in, Father. I have no doubt they're waiting for me in Warsaw. I will be cautious, and avoid them if they are. However, if they are there, I will then go home and join my mother in the next world. This world is no place for monsters like the vampire or like those of us, who hunt them.

"Father, I have come to you in hopes that your organization, one that has hunted demons for centuries, will understand the importance of the information contained in my journal. I do not ask you for absolution, for there can be no absolution for one such as I have become. I ask only that you take this journal, keep it safe, get it into the hands of the people in your church who will know what to do with it. Promise me you will do this."

"My son, you're wrong. Any man can be absolved by God, if he truly desires it and repents of his sins."

"But I don't, Father. I regret only that I didn't kill Melosh years ago for what he did to me, made me become. The men I've killed deserved to die; they were monsters like me. No, I ask only that you care for the journal. The information contained therein is hard won, written in the blood of many victims, both innocent and guilty.

"Father, the vampires truly do exist, they're demons from hell, and they must be hunted down and destroyed utterly, erased from the earth. Swear to me you will do this. Swear it by the god you serve. Place that journal in the hands of the men in your church, the secret orders that deal with such things. Swear it to me now."

"My son, the things you've told me have horrified me, especially that you have no regrets, and yet, I can hear the conviction in your voice. I will do as you ask of me, for the sake of your immortal soul." The priest waited, but there was no sound from the other side of the confessional. After a while he gave up and peeked inside. Johan was gone, but the leather bound journal was lying on the seat.

Hunted

Johan cautiously climbed out of the manhole, carefully checking the area before showing himself. Once again, he'd managed to elude the vampires, but only just. He made his way to a sheltered spot and settled down behind several rusty containers to wait for darkness to fall.

Melosh, that bastard was still alive. The vampires had captured him and obviously had him in thrall, probably used that voice of command on him. Well, the network was useless now. They'd know of every one of them, and Melosh had taken them right to the secret places. He knew he was on his own now.

Worse yet, he could no longer access the money. Obviously the vampires had commanded Melosh to give it all to them, the bank accounts were empty. These creatures were so powerful, how could anyone hope to defeat them?

Ah, but they had though, hadn't they? They'd caught her, he'd tightened the wires, heard her screams of pain. Yes, they could be defeated. The question now was, did he still want to? Had he ever truly wanted to?

With a sigh, Johan admitted to himself that had never been his great desire, it was Melosh's. He'd only been terrified, first by the vampire, and then by Melosh's burning passion for revenge. He wasn't even sure why he'd never run away, but he hadn't.

He'd stayed, learned, practiced, and slowly began to realize they had become worse than the beast they hunted. At least the vampire was driven by the need for blood. Yes, the mad creature that killed his family was completely insane, but was he any different? Was Melosh? He was certain Melosh would have laughed as he watched the boy dismember a vampire, if they had managed to catch one.

Johan sighed again then rose and cautiously approached his hidden car. The coast was clear, so he slipped inside and drove away. He had almost no money left, so Finland was out of the question, besides, he had no doubt the vampires would be there waiting for him.

No, there was only one place left he could go. Home. After all the long years he set his thoughts back to that place of horror and dreams of his mother. He would go home to that fearful place and join her; he would finally be reunited with his beloved mother. With that determination in mind, he drove northwest.

Johan drove on through much of the night, stopping only once to gaze at the stars and then to catch a short nap. By dawn he was nearing his goal. He stopped and spent the last of his money on food and fuel. It didn't matter really, even though the silver bullets had not had the desired effect on the vampire, one of them would serve his purpose well enough. By noon he reached the village.

THE PLANE LANDED JUST before the sun rose above the trees. The tarp was swiftly pulled over the vehicle, then they set out slowly. Eric went on ahead, and soon returned with an old farm truck. Everyone piled into the truck and endured the ride to the village. The sun was up, but only just when they arrived. The villagers were curious to see so many strangers arrive in a farm truck. Several of them were dressed in some sort of military uniform, and the rest were too well dressed to ride in such a vehicle.

A few cautiously approached, asking who they were and what they wanted. Gudrun told them they were trying to capture a serial killer who was reported to be headed this way. She described Johan and asked if anyone had seen him. They hadn't.

Melosh was brought forward. A few of the older people remembered him. He told them they were looking for the boy, Johan, who had survived the church fire with him so many years ago. No one had seen him. They then pointed out where the bodies from that time had been buried. It was clear that none of these villagers had seen what had happened at that time. All they could remember was the church burning and the screams of the dying.

Seeing the way everyone deferred to Rhonda, one old woman shyly approached, holding a faded old photograph in her hand. She bowed her head and spoke softly, catching Ella's attention. They spoke for a moment, the woman first pointing to the photograph and then at Rhonda. "Ella, what is she saying?"

"She says her grandmother was a servant of the Romanov family. She's pointing to the picture of the princess whose body was never found. She says you look like her and wants to know if you're related. What should I tell her?"

"Does she speak English?"

"No."

Rhonda smiled at the woman and spoke to her, reaching out to touch her arm gently. "Tell her the woman in the picture was my great grandmother, but she must not ever tell anyone. No one must ever know."

Ella translated and the old woman beamed her pleasure as she agreed to keep the secret. Rhonda pulled a silver ring from her hand and gave it to the woman with a wink. Wide-eyed, the woman clutched the ring in both hands and, bowing, slowly backed away then hurried home to hide her treasure.

"That was sweet, Highness."

"She was sweet, Ella. What harm can it do if she enjoys a fantasy, a connection to her grandmother's life?"

"None at all, Ronni. Here comes Gudrun."

"What's the good word?"

"We got here first, and they've shown us where the bodies were buried, but there could be a problem."

"Oh?"

"An old man told us that when they buried the remains after the fire, they tried to identify and put the maimed corpses together for a decent burial."

"Oh shit."

"Exactly, it seems that someone dug up one of the fresh graves. They never found out who did it, but the body was taken, and they couldn't understand why."

"So, somewhere out there we could have one of Mobutu's vampires still on the loose."

"Sadly, that is a possibility." Ella sighed. "Are we never to be rid of that madness?"

"That's a worry for another time. Right now, we need to be prepared for the current situation. Gudrun, what's your best guess of when our quarry should arrive?"

"Depending on when he left, he could arrive at noon or shortly after. We should get dug in."

"Where do you want me?"

"This way, Princess."

"Gudrun, don't make me slap you." Gudrun chuckled as she led the way. She led Rhonda to a small building near the graveyard.

"Shouldn't I be in the air?"

"Honey, we dare not take the chance of someone seeing you transform. You and Igor both need to stay in human form. On the bright side, this is only one man and not a shapeshifter nor a vampire. My guys will take him down. You put some thought into the next step."

"I've already got that planned."

"Oh?"

"We pick up this guy, then drop me off at the sanctuary with the prisoner. You take Melosh and round up a few more of the network, three or four should do it. Then we all go back to the castle where you were held prisoner. We set up the cameras, release them from the compulsion, Eric and crew mow them down, then help a weakened woman, wrapped in a blanket, into a car and leave.

"We leak all this to the police with a note saying these murderers captured the wrong woman, and her crew took her back. There is no actual evidence of a vampire anywhere, just footage of a woman being tortured. Her loyal soldiers came and rescued her. Humanity shakes its head in wonder at the madness of these murderers pretending to be vampire hunters. Everybody knows there's no such thing.

"Once all that's done, we go home. I hear Harald is planning to hold a party and embarrass me in public." She stopped speaking as a piercing whistle alerted them. Eric had sounded the alarm. As silent as a ghost, Gudrun faded away and vanished around a headstone.

THE OLD CAR ROLLED into the village and stopped. Johan got out and gazed all around, spotting the church. By the looks of it, it had been rebuilt soon after it burned to the ground. He was puzzled when the villagers shied away from him, but perhaps they could sense the monster lurking inside. That thought brought him little comfort as he began to walk among the headstones, seeking his mother's name.

He finally found her, and wept openly as he sank to his knees and pulled the pistol from his pocket, bringing it slowly to his temple. Johan was not to have his release, however. The gun was snatched from his hand by a powerfully built man who tossed it aside. He leaped to his feet to strike at the stranger.

The blow didn't land, but the stranger's fist did, several times. "Don't mark him up, Terry. He needs to be all pretty for the cameras." Johan didn't understand the language, but at the sound of the woman's voice, the man lowered his fists and stepped back.

"Who are you people? What do you want?"

"We're her people, and we want you dead," said a different woman, speaking in Russian.

He spun around to see her, the vampire he'd tortured, walking toward him in sunlight. She was so beautiful, flawless, showing no sign at all of the damage he'd inflicted on her. "This man is my husband, and he wants you dead, to kill you himself, but the princess has said no, she has a use for you as yet."

At that point Rhonda marched past him, Igor on her right and Ella on her left. "Bring him, Gudrun. We're done here."

Johan didn't understand his words, but he understood her tone, and what happened next. *"Follow that woman, obey her every command."* Fighting himself all the way, he stumbled along behind Rhonda. He was placed in the truck beside Melosh, who translated for the woman, and told him to stare at his hands. He did as he was told.

As the truck bumped along toward the place where they'd hidden the plane, Rhonda pulled out her phone and checked in with the king.

"Harald here."

"It's Ronni. Success, Sire. We now have both the leaders in our custody. It'll take us another few days to wrap this up then we'll come home."

"That's wonderful news, Ronni. When you come home, bring Peter, Victor, and Justine with you. The others are already on their way."

"Oh, are we having a party?"

"Don't play coy with me, young lady. By now you know damn well what's going on. Rhonda, I need to have an official heir. I'm sure by now that you know you're my first choice for this. Please say yes."

"Yes, my king, I'll accept the title, but you have to give me a dozen centuries or more before you abdicate. It'll take that long for Gudrun and Ella to get me trained."

"From what I've heard, you've already proven yourself, Ronni, but yes, that's a deal. Finish up what you need to do then come back to us, Lady Hawk, heir to the throne. We'll make it official, then things can get back to normal."

"Back to normal? We were at normal before?"

His roar of laughter brought a smile to her face. "Go back to work, Queen of the Werewolves."

"Yes, my king."

She was still smiling as the soldiers pulled the tarp from the plane and loaded everyone on board. Eric returned the farm truck then jogged back to the plane and settled into the pilot's seat. "Where to, Lady Hawk?"

"Back to the sanctuary, Eric. We'll catch a night's rest, then go from there." He nodded and pushed down on the controls. The plane rose up into the air, turned ninety degrees then shot away. Within an hour they were once more enjoying Peter's hospitality.

Plans

The prisoners were put in cells, then everyone gathered for a meal. When the meal was finished they sat back with tea, enjoying the fact they had managed to catch the elusive prey, the mad vampire hunter. "Have you reported your success to the king yet?"

"Yes, Ella, I checked in. He told me to finish up here then bring everybody with me when I come home. He officially asked me to be his heir."

"And what did you tell him?"

"I said I'd do it if he gives me a dozen centuries before he abdicates. It'll take me that long to get ready, learn what I need to know."

Ella chuckled at that. "So, what's the next step?"

"Next Gudrun and crew gather up a few men from that network, Victor gathers what we need to stage the final scene, and I spend some time with Illya and Anna."

"Oh? How can we serve, Queen Ronni?"

"Illya, my friend, my pack in America are mostly the children who were tortured. They didn't have a normal life. If I'm to lead all the wolves, I need to learn what a natural life for them is like, how the pups are raised, what do they learn, experience first, next, what do the elders teach? I need to know these things, so I can try to bring as much of that as possible into this modern world as I can for them, for the future generations."

"I have badly misjudged you, my queen."

"No, Illya, you want to restore the packs, so do I. You have the right idea; your reasoning is sound, and we'll proceed along those lines as much as possible."

"Thank you, Lady. Should I fetch Anna now?"

"Yes, please, and a few more of the elders as well. This night you all are the teachers and I'm the student." Smiling, he turned and left the room in search of the wolves.

"That was well done, Ronni."

"Thanks. Ella, I've got a difficult task for you, but there's no hurry."

"Oh? What is it? What do you need?"

"What we all need. I need to learn a few languages, so I can function better. I'd like to add German, French, and especially Russian. I also plan to ask Illya teach me the old language of the werewolves. I need you to remember a language from the past, something you could teach everybody, that no living human could know or understand."

Ella smiled with delight. "I'd enjoy that, Ronni. I understand your sudden need for languages. Harald would be your best bet for German, he was in Berlin for centuries. Marlene's a natural for French, and Peter or Victor for Russian, certainly."

"But?"

"But an ancient language?"

"Ella, you know all too well that we live in the age of intrusiveness. We always have to be watching out for listening devices. Every mission I've been on that's been a problem we watch for. Sometimes, they get past us, even if for a moment. If we all spoke a language that no one could understand but us ..."

Ella nodded, as she absorbed the possibilities. "I like it, but so much of our lives is caught up in modern technology, and that has a language of its own. Any language I could teach would have no way to reference a phone, text message, the internet, ..."

"I know, I know, but we can include the language of tech in what you teach. For example, "Enta briga doone text Gudrun, ot gambla eotka rathe internet site, ak lintor."

Ella was laughing heartily now. "All right, I see what you mean. Even if someone was listening in, that would drive them mad trying to break the code. You know, the way ancient hunter gatherers referenced the world around them could easily be applied to much of our world, but I think I'd like to move a bit closer to our own time."

"Oh?"

"Yes, there is a language I know quite well that will suit our purpose. There are a few humans who think they can understand it, but they have no real idea of how it actually sounds when spoken by a native speaker. It's the language Harald's people spoke when I first met him. Sometimes we speak it just to enjoy the memories. Torvil is somewhat familiar with it as well."

"That's perfect, so perfect. Oh, I just had a great idea. Did Harald's people use horses?"

"Yes, at least the nobility did, why?"

"When, do you think, was the last time King Harald rode out with hawk and hound?"

"Centuries past, it was his favorite pastime before he was made vampire, and he hasn't done it much since as far as I know. Ronni, what are you ...? Oh my lord, you're not thinking ..."

"Yes I am. I'll have to talk Igor and Derek into helping me. What do you think, is it a good idea or not?"

"I think it's a wonderful idea and I think he'll love it if you can make it happen."

"Oh, I'll make it happen, but I'll need your help, you and Queen Sally."

"What do you want us to do?"

"I want you to steal that old saddle the king keeps in his training area."

"Oh yes, we can do that. I'll talk to Sally as soon as we get back. Ah, here comes Gudrun."

Gudrun strode up to them, smiling, confident, every bit her old self. She lightly kissed Rhonda's hair then sat. "Me and the boys are on our way to Helsinki. My people have captured three of the vampire hunters who live there. Is that enough for what you have planned?"

"It is. Bring them back here, Ella can put the compulsion on all of them, then we'll head back to that accursed castle and get this done. Once we have that filmed, Heinrich can float it to the proper authorities, and they can make an end of that vampire hunting network for us. Then we go home."

"I like it, Ronni. So, you two look like you're up to mischief, what's going on?"

"We're plotting against the king," said Ella, grinning with delight. "We'll tell you all about it when you get back."

"Oh gods, the suspense. I guess I'd better get on the go and get this done then. With your permission, Highness."

Rhonda pointed toward the door, trying to look fierce. "Go. Don't make me slap you."

With a small bow and a chuckle of delight, Gudrun rose and strode away. Rhonda watched her go with misty eyes. "Ronni?"

"It's so good to see her back to her old self, Ella. She was so hurt, so tortured."

"Yes, but you saved her, brought her back to us. You made it right, Lady Hawk."

"I'm in awe of her strength and self-control. That's one of the things she's going to have to teach me."

"Ronni?"

"Johan and Melosh, Ella, they're both still alive. I can assure you, if that had been me being tortured, they wouldn't be."

"Nor will they be for much longer."

"No, but Gudrun's held herself in check. She's interrogated them, but hasn't ... Somehow I need to develop that kind of discipline."

"All in good time, Highness. All in good time. Here comes Illya now, with Anna and a few of the elders. Time for you to tend to your people now."

Ella lightly patted Rhonda's hand then moved away to let the others sit closer to their queen. She found Igor with Heinrich, planning out the final stage of the film they wanted to release to the authorities.

IT WAS ONLY A SHORT while later, while she was speaking with the elders, Rhonda's phone buzzed insistently. She glanced down to see it was the king. "Harald?"

"Ronni, the Russian military is almost at your door."

"Dammit. Understood, my king."

The connection broke and Rhonda was instantly on her feet, calling for Peter and Igor. Igor was first to reach her. "Ronni?"

"We've got incoming, military. Take the wolves into the forest, all of them. I'll find you where we make our last kill. Igor, take Ella with you. Go!" Igor sped away, calling for the wolves.

Peter came hurrying toward Rhonda. "Peter, tell me you have an emergency evacuation plan."

"We do, Highness. What's happening?"

"Russian military. The wolves are in the forest, you get your people out. Go to Finland or the sanctuary in Germany."

"Be at peace, Highness. We're prepared for something like this. We'll get you to safety then deal with this."

"Don't worry about me, Peter, I'll be in the forest with the wolves. You do your thing." She raced to the door and leaped toward the sky with a piercing call.

Less than an hour later two military trucks rumbled up to the compound. The Lady Hawk lay on the updraft and watch from above as two men in hunter's garb climbed out of the truck with the soldiers. She silently berated herself for her impetuous action in showing herself before. Her eyes widened as Peter, dressed in a Russian military uniform, bedecked with dozens of medals, stepped out of the building. Victor was beside him in a business suit.

The commander of the military saluted Peter then spoke. Peter replied, then stepped aside to invite him inside. Rhonda cursed silently and redoubled her vow to learn Russian. The soldiers left in the yard looked Justine over as she accompanied Victor outside. They distributed face masks to the soldiers who hesitated, then, as Victor spoke to them, put them on.

Soon after, the commander and Peter reappeared with Heinrich checking some sort of instrument. He spoke then removed his own mask. The others followed his example, then the military placed the two hunters in restraints, got back in their truck, and drove away.

Once they were out of sight, Victor looked up and gave Rhonda the thumbs up salute. She gave a piercing call then flew off, but soon returned with the wolf pack and tigress. Lidiya was waiting with clothing for them all.

"Peter, what happened?"

"We put our contingency plan into action, and I'm pleased to say, it worked well. I invited the commander inside, explained to him we were doing secret experiments with hallucinogens, put the compulsion on him so he fully believed it. Victor and Justine took the masks out to the soldiers and told them the same and to wear the masks until we got the leak sealed.

"The result is, the two men are now convinced they were under the influence of drugs, the local military commander will now ignore any other reports about this place, and we can go about our business as usual."

"So, you were prepared for something like this. I got the warning and I panicked. Dammit, I should have known you would have everything under control."

"Actually, Highness, I believe you handled the situation perfectly."

"Oh?"

"Yes. You instinctively took the best action to get your people to safety, then when I said we had a plan for this, you didn't argue, you didn't question, you accepted that I could deal with it and turned back to the protection of the wolves, your chosen people."

"Peter, all the non-humans are my chosen people, but yes, I get your meaning. So, we're clear now?"

"We are, Highness."

Rhonda sighed and let her shoulders relax. "What would you have done had I not been here? How would you explain all the people and the prisoners?"

"I wouldn't. Highness, that man got no further into this facility than the reception area, although he believes he has seen everything. In his mind, most of the building, and the prison cells, have been closed off."

"But they haven't, have they?"

"No. Should the soldiers break in, we would withdraw into the prison corridors, shutting all automatic doors behind us. We would then evacuate through the secret tunnel we created ourselves."

"Created yourselves? Peter, you've only been here a bit over a year, how ...?"

"This place was one of Gudrun's hideouts, part of her safety net from her mercenary days. She hired a number of former military engineers to create the tunnel then put them under the compulsion to make them think they were actually closing off and sealing the prison. When we arrived, we opened it up and the wolves have been using it as an access point to the forest.

"We also have the cells prepared in case we have to house a non-human who cannot function openly. We have none as yet, but I know the king has at least two or three.

"Highness, we can easily escape this place if we have to and set a self-destruct if necessary. Heinrich has redundant back-ups in secure places. I believe this place to now be as secure as the Lair, the castle in Germany as well.

"Lady, I had planned to give you a full tour of the facility and a complete rundown of our security measures. Unfortunately, it was another matter that brought you to us and held your, all our, attention. You had no way to know."

Rhonda chuckled and patted his arm. "Thanks for letting me off the hook so easily, Peter, but I know I messed up here, big time. First, I lost my temper and showed myself, that brought the military to us. Second, as soon as we arrived I should have asked you for the full story on this place."

"We all make mistakes, Highness. You've been chosen to climb a steep learning curve, and I'm quite impressed with how well you're doing. Lady, you instantly sent your wolves to safety, then when I said we had things well in hand, you didn't argue that, or try to take control, you accepted my word and trusted me to deal with the emergency.

"However, I did notice a hawk in the sky keeping an eye on things. You saw your people to safety, then remained close in case I might need you. I grow more and more impressed with Harald's choice of heir. With Harald on the throne and you as the heir, the kingdom is in good hands. I'm feeling quite secure in that."

"Thank you, Peter, the princess's feelings are soothed, but I need you to know something, all of you. It's okay to tell me when I screw up. You all have much to teach, and I do want to learn, I need to learn. I can't afford to make mistakes like that again."

Ella stepped closer and put her arm around Rhonda's shoulders. "You're being too hard on yourself, Ronni. Peter's right, we all make mistakes, in fact, both Peter and I have made a goodly number ourselves. It's the nature of life. The key here, is to learn from each one so we don't end up repeating them. Relax, disaster has been averted, all is well."

"Yes, mom," sighed Rhonda, as she eased the tension in her shoulders. "Thanks for saving my butt, all of you." There were smiles all round, but no one spoke. "I should let Harald know we survived."

A Fighting Chance

Rhonda reported to the king then returned to her session with the wolf elders. She was surprised to learn they had mostly lived as humans, maintaining comfortable homes deep in the mountains. They spent the winters in broad valleys, but in spring returned to the high reaches, close to the tree line.

The main difference was their lack of agriculture. Instead, they hunted and gathered, relying heavily on the hunting. They had also developed ways of preserving meat, cooking it with herbs and roots they found in the forest. They would move from one small settlement to another about three times a year. Once each year they'd gather for a festival, a gathering of the packs. It was at one such event that they had been decimated by the criminal mastermind, Stephan Krebs.

Their clothing was mostly made of leather with some articles made of tightly woven grasses. It was mostly long tunics, leggings, boots, and heavy cloaks made of furs. Rhonda sat smiling as she listened to the stories of days spent in warm sun and deep forests. She asked Nikka to learn as much as possible of the skills and stories they could teach, so she could return to the Lair to teach the others in turn.

They were still at it when Gudrun and crew returned. She came striding into the room, a smile on her face. She stopped in front of Rhonda, giving her a slight bow. Rhonda shook her finger at her. "Everything under control?"

"It is, Ronni. Those men have been put in the cells with Melosh and Johan. It's getting a bit late tonight for this. We should wait until sundown tomorrow before we do this."

Rhonda nodded her agreement. "Fair enough, but I want to talk to all of them. I want them to know what's coming and why." She started to turn toward the cells, but Terry Sawchuk was in her path. "Terry?"

"Ronni, let me."

"Proper respect, husband ..."

"Gudrun, it's all right. Terry?"

"Ronni, I need to do this. They took her, tortured ..."

"Easy now, Terry, easy. I get it. Got a plan?"

"Ronni, I know what you want done here. I like it. I've talked to Eric and the guys; we want to do the nasty, and we want them to know what's coming. Please, let me do this."

Rhonda smiled and patted his shoulder. "All yours, boss. Go lay it out for them. Mind if I listen in?"

"Not at all."

He turned and led the way to the cells. Rhonda followed with Igor at her side, Gudrun and Ella close behind. Terry stopped at the barred door that separated him from Johan. "Can any of you scum suckers speak English?" No one twitched a muscle.

"Are they all under the compulsion?"

"Yes, my husband, they're all enthralled. Do you want them let loose?"

"Please, Goody."

"*Listen carefully, you are all released from compelled instruction, but only for the moment.*" Gudrun repeated the message in Russian and Finnish. Slowly, the men shook off the spell and fearfully took in their surroundings. "Go ahead, lover. I'll translate for you."

Terry nodded then spoke, pausing often to allow Gudrun to translate. "Pay attention. You men are all murders and worse. There are those among us who would like to give you a full dose of your own medicine, but the princess says no, you will not be tortured. However, you are to get a chance for life. There are five of you, you will face four men, me and three others.

"Your weapons will be returned to you, tranquilizer rounds and silver bullets as well as the heavy nets. You will be returned to the place where you held and tortured this woman. There you will face us in combat. If you defeat us or escape, you live. If not, you suffer the fate you planned for her. You get a fighting chance, more than you gave her or any of your other victims."

Fighting to get his rage under control, Terry pointed a finger at Johan, then turned and walked away, followed by the others.

They watched their captor walk away then Melosh spoke. "You left me there, Johan, you traitorous coward. You left me to face the vampires alone and you ran like frightened child."

"I did, and I have no regrets for the act. I should have done that forty years ago, left you there in your own blood and the blood of my family. I should have run from the madness in your eyes, gone to my uncle, and lived a normal life.

"You used me, Melosh. You took a frightened child and molded him into a weapon, made him a monster like the one we hunted. Yes, I left you there as I should have long ago. I hoped the vampire would finish you, for I had not the courage to do it myself."

"I raised you as my own, Johan. You were a son to me."

"I was a tool for you, Melosh, a tool with which to hunt and hurt the vampire, nothing more. Know this, when they return our weapons I will kill you first, then face their guns with open arms."

"No!" said one of the other men. "You came to me, to us, convinced us to help you hunt the vampire. You helped us capture them and taught us to torture and kill them as well as other men. The only chance we have to survive is to work together. First we survive this, then, and only then, you can finish this thing between you. You owe us that much."

Johan gazed at the man for a long moment then slowly nodded his head. "Very well then, we survive, then I will leave you all behind." He turned away and sat on the bed, staring into space and refused to respond to anything further.

Melosh turned to the other men and spoke softly. "Johan has always been weak, but I can no longer hold him up. You'll have to watch him, and not depend on him to be of much use in the battle." They nodded, but Johan gave no indication if he heard.

BACK IN THE WAR ROOM, Rhonda lightly gripped Terry's arm. "You offer them a fighting chance? Why Terry?"

"Yes. Don't worry, Ronni, they won't survive. They'll pay with their lives for what they did to Goody."

"Why, Terry? No bullshit now, tell me why?"

He wouldn't make eye contact. It was Gudrun who answered her question. "He doesn't want you to have to give the order, honey. You could take those guys out in battle, but he knows you and knows it would tear you apart to set them up then slaughter them."

Rhonda straightened at that. "Then your husband seriously underestimates my outrage at what was done to you, and he underestimates my resolve to see them dead because of it. If they'd been working alone, they'd already have gone to meet their maker, but their network must be destroyed with them. They and their network are a threat to all my people, and I need to remove that threat."

"Easy, my pretty bird, easy. Mr. Terry is not the enemy here."

Rhonda sighed and let her shoulders relax. "No, he's not. Sorry, Terry. You're right, this is wearing on me, and I appreciate the effort to lighten the load for me."

"I do have an issue here, too."

"I know you do, Terry. You may have offered them a fighting chance, but I promise you, even if they escape the castle, they will not survive. I'll be right outside with a pack of wolves.

"Heinrich, is all in readiness?"

"It is, Highness. I'll be recording the battle, and I'll plant all the evidence for the police to find. As soon as we leave, I'll make an anonymous call to tip them off. They'll find the evidence, the bodies, and then they can finish cleaning up the network for us."

"There is one small issue," said Victor.

"Oh?"

"Johan's journal, it wasn't found with him or in the car. He must have hidden it somewhere."

"Well shit, that throws a wrench in the works."

Victor just grinned. "It's only a small detail, Highness. Let me go ask Johan where he left it then retrieve it for you."

Rhonda favored him with a wan smile. "You're a genius and a treasure, Victor." He beamed his pleasure at her praise.

"All right, folks, it's late and we need to get some rest. Tomorrow is D-day. Once we get this put to rest, we go home. I hear the king is planning a party." She rose, and everyone stood as Igor took her arm and led her away to their rest.

Once Rhonda was out of the room the others sat back down. Gudrun smiled at her husband. "What?"

"Did you learn what you wanted to know?"

"Yeah, I did, Goody. She's tougher than I thought."

"I told you."

"Yeah, I forget you guys are linked now, too."

"It's more than that, Terry. I knew it when she came for me, before she fed me, marked me. It was in her eyes, the rage at what was done, the compassion for me, and the determination to set it all right. She was in control though, and clearly in command.

"Terry, she appreciates that your desire to do this is as great or greater than her own. She can feel us, my connection to you, your connection to me. She knows you tested her a bit by giving her a way out, and perhaps a year or two ago she might have taken it, but not now.

"She's a lot stronger now, sweetie. The young hawk we tried to mentor has grown. Now she needs our support. Lady Hawk will make a fine leader. In truth, she's already become that. Harald's made the right choice here. You can relax, my lover, our Ronni isn't afraid to make the tough decisions anymore."

"So, our little bird is all grown up?"

"Ah-huh, and is now officially the queen of the werewolves, as well as the king's choice as heir to his throne."

"Yeah, well, it wasn't all about protecting her from the hard decision, nor was it all about testing her resolve. It was more about how bad I want those fuckers to know they're going to die for what they did, to know that I'm coming for them."

"I know, sweetie. Now for the hard part."

"What?"

"Tomorrow, I need you to do exactly as Eric tells you, no hesitation, and no free thinking. Terry, Eric is one of the most dangerous and able soldiers I've ever known. You've offered those bastards live ammo. I don't like it; things can all too often go wrong. Following Eric's orders gives you the best chance of staying alive. Promise me now."

"All right, Goody, it makes sense to give Eric the lead, the man has mad skills. Come on, let's get some rest."

Late the next day they set out. The plane was full, the warriors, the vampire hunters, Gudrun, Ella, Victor, and Rhonda plus Heinrich. Under the influence of the compulsion, the hunters sat staring at their hands as commanded. The plane landed at the base of the castle hill, and the men were marched up to the castle, the original computer was re-installed, as was the camera. The men were given their weapons then released from the compulsion.

Shaking off the spell, they swiftly armed themselves then took up defensive positions, defending the open gate. They waited, and waited, but nothing happened. "Where are they?"

"They're playing with us," said Melosh. "They will come, we will use our training against them. Once we defeat them we will be free."

"Do you truly expect them to honor that agreement?" asked one of the men.

"They will if we capture the short one alive," replied Johan. "That one is the vampire's mate. Obviously, the sunlight does them no harm.

The only thing we know for certain is that cutting off the head is the final end for them.

"We must capture the mate alive but hold him captive with a blade at his throat. In this way we can force them to live up to the agreement. When they come, focus your efforts on the short vampire." They nodded their agreement and settled in to wait.

It was two long hours later and their nerves were frayed. Suddenly one man hissed a warning. He'd spotted movement on the hill leading to the castle gate. They all strained to pierce the gloom with their eyes, then the flash grenade popped, effectively blinding them.

There was the rattle of gunfire even before they cleared their vision. It came from the side. Two men were already down when the lights came up, bathing the entire courtyard with bright light. They'd somehow gotten inside without being seen.

The remaining three swiftly took cover from this attack. Jimmy settled to the ground behind some rubble, swearing profusely as he plucked a tranquilizer dart from his neck. Vassily grinned at him as he did a diving roll past an open spot to hide behind another pile of rubble. He waited only a moment then made another run, drawing the enemy fire and all the attention.

Focused on Vassily, they didn't see Terry and Eric enter through the open gate. Two quick, well-placed, shots from Eric's gun and only Johan remained alive. Slowly, he rose to his feet to see Terry facing him. He watched as Terry tossed aside his weapon, then motioned for him to come out.

Checking the hidden blade up his sleeve, Johan nodded. Perhaps he could yet take a vampire to the other side with him. One way or the other he would join his mother before the sun rose in the sky. It was what he wanted.

Johan tossed aside his rifle as he stepped forward to meet Terry. "Come, vampire. Let us make an end of this, you and I."

Terry had no idea what he'd said, nor did he care. He moved in quickly but dodged aside as the blade appeared in Johan's hand. Terry's speed saved him from a killing stroke, but he was cut deeply. Johan spun toward him, but he was faster and delivered a savage kick to the man's knee. With a grunt of pain Johan stumbled. The second kick struck his wrist, knocking the knife free.

They struggled for the knife, but Terry was losing blood, and it was costing him. He let go and rolled away. As Johan retrieved the knife and tried to stand, Terry spun on his back and delivered another kick, this time to the other knee. With a howl of pain Johan pitched forward, falling on the blade he'd meant for another man's heart.

As his life ebbed, he smiled. He didn't see the battlefield, nor did he feel the pain. Instead, he saw his mother smile and reach for him. "Come Johan, we will gaze at the stars together." The peace he'd longed for and could never find, finally settled on his countenance as life left his body.

"Jimmy, Terry needs to be patched up, Vassily and I'll find Gudrun." As Jimmy hurried to Terry's side with his med kit, Eric and Vassily moved off camera. Terry, sporting fresh bandages, was back on his feet as Eric walked back across the camera's field of vision, carrying a woman wrapped up in a blanket. Only her golden hair could be seen on camera.

Terry leaned on Jimmy as they followed Eric carrying Gudrun out the gate. As soon as they were far enough away she leaped from Eric's arms and ran to Terry. "Dammit all, husband. Hand to hand? Seriously? How many times do I have to tell you, if you want to kill a man and you have a gun, use it."

"Beat me up later, sweetheart, when I'm revived enough to enjoy it."

High overhead, the hawk gave a piercing cry then swooped down to meet them at the plane. Soon Heinrich came out of the castle, and the wolves came out of the forest. "It's all set to go, Lady Hawk. Once we're well away I'll make that call."

"Thank you, Heinrich. Well done. Gudrun, how's Terry?"

"Not good, Ronni."

"You must have a contingency plan for things like this. If he needs a hospital ..."

"He does. We have one in Denmark ..."

"No, there's no time ..." He tried to say more, but Gudrun hushed him.

"Fine then," said Rhonda, "are we all here?"

"We are Highness."

"Eric, get us back to the Russian sanctuary as quickly as possible. Heinrich, contact Justine, tell her we're coming in fast with wounded. We need the infirmary prepped."

"At once, Highness."

"Ronni?"

"Justine and I are both veterinarians, Gudrun. We'll patch him up for you, then you can take him to your people once we have him fully stabilized."

Gudrun closed her eyes and drew a deep breath, then slowly released it. "Ronni, I ..."

"Relax, sister, Jimmy's got him patched up, but he'll need stitches and a few meals of red wine and rare steak. It looked worse than it was." She moved Terry's shirt back into place.

Gudrun kissed Rhonda's cheek then turned her attention to Terry. "Listen buddy, if you ever risk your life with that macho shit again, I'll ..."

"Not my fault, bastard was left-handed."

Tears filled her eyes as she smacked his forehead with her finger. "Shut up, Terry, just shut up and let me fuss over you." He smiled and squeezed her hand. She shuddered at how weak his grip was.

Rhonda made her way to the cockpit. "Eric, how're we doing?"

"Touchdown in five, Ronni. They're waiting with a stretcher. Justine contacted the Lair, got the goods on Terry, and has a blood donor waiting." She nodded her approval, patted his shoulder, then returned to her seat to cuddle into Igor who snuggled her close.

The plane lightly touched down. As the door opened, Peter and Justine were waiting with a stretcher and soon had Terry in the lab. He was fading in and out of consciousness at this point. Justine gave him a shot and he relaxed. A short while to let it take hold, then another local before she and Rhonda stitched up the two major cuts.

Lidiya stood by, silently waiting. "Will he need blood?"

"He probably should have it. Are you the donor?"

"I am, Highness."

"What do you think, J?"

Justine sighed and put aside her stethoscope. "I'd like to give him some, Ronni."

"All right then, let's do it."

ELLA HAD TAKEN GUDRUN to the dining hall. "Both Ronni and Justine are trained medical people, they know what they're doing. Come on, we'll sit here and drink too much coffee while we wait."

"Yeah, I know you're right, Mother, but ... Dammit, what the hell possessed him to engage in hand to hand when he had a perfectly serviceable automatic weapon in his hand?"

"I don't know what to tell you, Gudrun. I'm over a million years old, and I still don't understand men."

"It's not so hard," said Igor as he joined them. "That man tortured you; Terry wanted to hurt him, slowly, make him suffer for what he did. He wanted to defend his mate in a challenge of combat, to prove himself worthy."

"Prove himself worthy? Seriously?"

"Yes, Miss Gudrun. You are stronger, faster, and so Terry feels the need to be worthy of that, to show you that you have chosen a strong mate, a mate who is strong enough to defend you."

"And this makes sense to you."

"Of course. Anyone can see it." Both women looked at each other with raised eyebrows, then turned to him.

Igor was saved by Rhonda's return. She kissed Gudrun's cheek and sighed. "There's some guy in the infirmary who's going to need a lot of babying for the next couple of weeks, but he'll be fine. He got cut up a bit, but no vital organs were hit, just muscle. We stitched him up, Lidiya donated a couple of pints of the good stuff, and Justine's sitting with him until he wakes up. Shouldn't be long."

"Ronni, I ..."

"Go on now, go relieve Justine. He'll want to see your face when he wakes up. He'll be fine, my sister, but you'll have to hold him down for a while until he's healed fully." Gudrun kissed Rhonda's cheek, hugged her tightly for a moment, then fled to the infirmary.

At this point Heinrich joined them. "I love technology," he grinned.

"Oh?"

"Yes, Highness. Apparently, my phone call was unnecessary. Some of the folk from the village reported the sound of gunfire. The Finnish authorities were already on their way to the village before I called. The news reports are already on the internet."

"Do tell."

"Oh yes. It seems there is a group of murderers operating out of such places. The police of several countries are joining forces to hunt them down."

"At last," sighed Rhonda. "Okay, guess I'd better report to the king, let him know we'll soon be on the way home."

Peter arrived to join them. "In a hurry to get home, Highness?"

"Yes and no, Peter. Yes, I want to get home, rest in my own bed, and take a day or two to absorb all that's happened. However, I find myself somewhat reluctant to leave this place, and all the new friends I've made, behind. I want to come back for a proper visit, have a chance to spend time with all of you when we're not under the gun. You know what I mean?"

"I do, Highness, and I'm delighted to hear it. We'll set up a proper royal suite for you, so you can visit whenever you wish. There's still a lot of this place you haven't had a chance to inspect."

"And I do want to see it. Alas, I fear the king is getting anxious. I think he's afraid I'll chicken out." That brought a round of chuckles.

WHILE THE HEIR TO THE throne and her people relaxed, and her sister held her wounded husband and gently wept, five men sat in a private meeting room. All were in official looking uniforms. "Are you certain?" asked one.

"I am," came the answer. "See here, the torture of this woman, there, her face, you see? That's Gudrun Arielsdottir, the mercenary."

"The angel of death? How in the name of all that's holy did they manage to capture her?"

"I have no idea, but it was a fatal mistake. See here, at the end of the film, these men in uniform, those are her men. This one, Eric Hansen of Denmark, next to Gudrun herself, probably the most dangerous soldier on the planet."

"I know that man," said another. "That's an American CIA agent who went rogue a couple of years ago and disappeared. Gentlemen, if these people go after the men listed on that computer, they're as good as dead already."

"She will go after them. The angel will not forgive torture like that."

"Do you think she survived it? Could anyone?"

"It doesn't matter," said another. "Rumor has it she is married to the American, and it is well known Hansen has a passion for her. If she dies of her wounds they will continue the hunt. These are not forgiving men. She's hurt, they'll wait to see if she will recover before they act. This gives us a small window of opportunity."

"I don't understand."

"We have to find these men swiftly. I for one, do not want our own people to be caught in the way when her strike force comes for one of those men. No, our only hope is to apprehend them first and quickly. If we do, perhaps they'll back off. They have, after all, eliminated the two ring leaders."

The others nodded their agreement, then phones began to ring as they put out the word. Find these men, quickly.

The Gathering

Rhonda awoke with a start, sitting up in the bed. "Ronni? What?"
"Gudrun. Terry's in trouble. Go wake Eric, tell him to prep the plane." With that she was out of the bed and out the door, tying a robe about her waist as she went. She was nearly to the infirmary when she encountered Gudrun coming the other way.

"Ronni ..."

"I've sent Igor to find Eric. He'll get the plane ready. Call your people in Denmark, have them waiting." She patted Gudrun's arm as she passed on her way by.

Rhonda swept into the infirmary to find Justine already there. "How's he doing, J?"

"He's got a bit of a fever, not an issue if we had the right antibiotics, but, something's not quite right. I'm thinking we should send him to a real hospital, just in case that damned blade was poisoned, or at least contaminated with something."

"Already in the works. Eric's prepping the plane as we speak. Come on, Terry, up and at 'em. We'll shift you onto the stretcher then give you a ride to the plane."

Gudrun returned and took the head of the stretcher, pulling it along easily as she steered it through the complex to the waiting plane outside. They loaded him aboard, then the big bird lifted off and vanished into the rising sun. "He needed to be transported?"

"Not certain really, Peter. I'm sure he'd have been fine here, but it can't hurt, and she'll feel better if she can make things happen for him. We'll have a day to ourselves, and it looks like I'll get that grand tour after all. Once the plane returns for us we'll go home and face the music."

"Face the music?"

"Peter, my friend, don't mistake me here, I'm enjoying being treated like a princess. It's fun and all, but I'm no fool, I know full well the responsibility that goes with the title."

"And yet you accepted."

"I was marginalized much of my life, told not to reach too high, to listen and be quiet when men speak. I can't tell you how many times I did things a certain way because it would cause too much trouble if I didn't, even though I could easily see a better way. Because I'm small of stature, men often spoke over me, or ignored my input completely.

"I've been chastised for trying to take control, even though to step back would mean the failure of a project. That's why I was out in the back roads the day I was changed, cleaning up a mess that should never have happen, but we did it the boss's way instead of the right way.

"Peter, all that stopped the day I was taken in by the non-humans. Since being welcomed by these people, I've been respected, loved, encouraged, trusted, and have had my opinions genuinely heard, taken into consideration.

"I fully believe I have something to offer, and if the king himself thinks I'm the right one for the job, then I'm willing to give it my all. Having said that, I'll admit I'm scared to death, and I do feel the weight of the responsibility, but I'm determined to succeed here, to nurture and protect our people, my chosen people, the people who took me in and gave me a better life. I'll do all in my power to make life better for them too."

Peter smiled as he listened. "Highness, I have no doubt at all that you will succeed, and as one of your subjects, I find this most encouraging. I fully believe the people will survive and thrive with you and Harald to lead us into the future. Come, I can smell the coffee from here." Rhonda chuckled as Igor took her arm and they accompanied Peter to the dining hall.

They found Heinrich there, having coffee and flirting with Justine. Once everyone was seated again, Rhonda turned to the sanctuary's electronics wizard. "So, Heinrich, what's the good word?"

"We live in a fast-paced world, Highness. Already the five training facilities have been swarmed by police, and several men have been arrested. Of our list, only eight men remain at large. Three of the seven safe houses have been raided as well.

"I believe we can safely say the vampire hunter's network has been demolished, but I will continue to monitor things carefully."

"I can see that you've got the situation well in hand."

She was grinning, and Justine blushed. "Shut up, Ronni. God, you're awful. I should have chewed your leg off when you carried me up onto that turret at the Lair."

Rhonda laughed at that. "I thought you were going to. I was trying to be all stern, but calm, ready to talk things out, but you went all berserk mouse on me. Scared me half to death."

"Oh bullshit. Actually, I thought you were going to leave me up there."

"I was afraid to. Heinrich, my friend, this is the mouse who roars, a fierce and savage warrior."

"Thank you, Highness, that is good to know. I am well forewarned."

"You're both pushing your luck, you know that."

Again, Rhonda chuckled. "Justine, you're amazing. I could never have gotten Gudrun back without you. You should have seen her. First, she disabled the cameras, then cut the wire off Gudrun, pulled her off before she drank me dry, and then she decked one of the guards and dragged him over for Gudrun to feed on."

"Ronni ..."

"I mean it, J. I couldn't have gotten her back without you. I owe you a big one."

Justine suddenly grinned with mischief. "Does that mean I get to kiss Igor again?"

"You do and I'll deck you, woman. You keep your hands off my guy."

At that Igor rose from the chair. "Heinrich, you promised to show me that new computer set up. How about now?"

"Yes, of course, but ..."

"My friend, if we stay here they will continue until we are both dead of embarrassment. Come, let us make good our escape." Rhonda and Justine sat grinning as the two men walked away.

"Thanks for that, Ronni."

"The mood getting a bit heavy, was it?"

"Just a bit. I've gotten over the Igor infatuation, but I'm not quite ready to leap into anything too heavy right now. I've got lots of new and exciting things to learn, experience, and I want to take a bit more time to enjoy that."

"I get that, but I wonder about something."

"Oh?"

"Well, when my hawk got broody, I was a goner. Igor's alpha was rising at the same time and bam! Both the wolf and hawk mate for life ..."

"But a mouse doesn't, add in my natural sex drives and, yes, every few weeks I can get a bit crazy. Poor Heinrich. I've tried to explain it to him, but I don't think he gets it yet."

"You run hot and cold on him?"

"Yeah, one week I'm just all over the sexy, then not so much. Try to convince a man that it's the natural rhythm of the mouse. I make him crazy, and I know it. I mean, you saw it. When you guys first landed I could have eaten Igor alive, you too for that matter, but a couple of days later ..."

"Well I'll be danged, so that was it. Woman you startled the hell out of me. When you threatened to kiss me, I didn't know if I should grab you or smack you. On the bright side, Ella assures me that, with time we settle into those rhythms and get full control."

"So we're going through puberty again?"

"Ah-huh."

"Well that really sucks."

Rhonda laughed with delight. "It truly does, my sister, it truly does. Come on, Peter's promised me a tour of the lesser known goodies of this sanctuary."

WHILE RHONDA ENJOYED her tour, Gudrun was talking with the doctor. "I'm impressed, Gudrun. You don't usually bring me people in such good shape. Whoever your new field medic is, they've done a wonderful job. If I didn't know better, I'd say those stitches were done by a well experienced surgeon. However, that fever has me a bit concerned. We'll give him a course of antibiotics, but I want to hold him for a few days, just to be sure. It was a knife wound, you say? I wonder if that blade may have been poisoned."

"Knowing what I know of that enemy, it very well may have been. Take every precaution, investigate every possibility, double check everything."

"This man is special to you?"

"My husband, and yes, he is precious to me."

"Well, not to worry. He should be ready for action in a couple of weeks. We'll investigate every possibility, I promise. We'll move him to the private suite, so you can settle in with him."

While Terry was being moved to the private room, Eric took the plane and headed out for Germany where he picked up passengers before moving on to Russia. Everybody was tired, so it was late the next day before they set out again. A long flight, then a refueling stop in England, and on again across the polar route to home. They arrived at the Lair with the rising sun. It was a busy place.

As they disembarked from the plane, Rhonda found herself being hugged, first by the king, and then by Sally. Everyone was greeted warmly and shown to their rooms to rest. As they settled down for a nap, Igor pulled Rhonda to him and kissed her gently. "What is it, sweet Ronni?"

"Hmm?"

"You're distracted. What is it?"

"The king. He's up to something."

"Ronni?"

"I've gotten to know this man a lot better over the past few months, Igor. He shows the world the strong decisive leader, but there's a fun-loving mischief maker hiding in there too. Harald enjoys a good joke, and he can be a bit of a tease. You can see it when he talks to Tanya."

"Da. Mr. Torvil told me that, in the olden times, the court jester could tease the king and get away with it. The jester could also say outrageous things and the king would always forgive. He says that our Tanya has taken on that role for King Harald, and the king likes it. Perhaps she gives him a chance to let out some of what you've seen."

"Yeah, I can understand that easily. Still, that doesn't help. Harald is up to something."

"Da, but so are we."

Rhonda giggled. "I know, but that's different."

"Stop this now, my pretty bird. Stop fussing and pay attention to your husband."

"My husband? Is my big bad wolf feeling neglected?"

"Terribly."

"Hmm, I'll see what I can do to take his mind off his troubles." She pushed him onto his back, straddled his chest, and kissed him deeply.

RHONDA AND IGOR ENTERED the dining hall just past noon. To her great surprise and embarrassment, Charles the butler stepped up beside them and spoke in a clear ringing voice. "Announcing Her Majesty, Lady Hawk, Queen of the Werewolves."

Rhonda's face blushed crimson as, with wide eyes, she and Igor were led to the two chairs at the king's immediate left. Everyone except the king and queen had risen. As she sat, the others did as well. "I'm sorry, Rhonda," grinned the king, "I know this is a bit formal, but the occasion calls for it. After this afternoon we'll take things back to the way they were."

She just gazed at him with those big eyes. She looked terrified. His grin widened as he pointed at the plate that had magically appeared before her. "Try the salmon, chef has outdone himself today."

Rhonda swallowed hard and brought her gaze to the plate. Beside her Igor chuckled. "You were right, my delight, the king was indeed up to something."

She didn't reply, just reached for a fork, but there were options. A quick glance across the table showed Ella watching her carefully. Once they made eye contact, Ella winked, then slowly reached for a fork. Throughout the meal Rhonda watched Ella carefully and followed her example.

At length the king arose. "Hear me, my people. We will gather in the great hall in three hours. There is to be an announcement of great importance. I know that not a single one of you has any idea at all of what's going on, but all shall soon be revealed." There was a round of chuckles as he took Sally by the arm and walked away.

Everyone had risen as the king and queen left, but they sat back down again. Rhonda slowly resumed her chair, still wide eyed. Ella made eye-contact again and gently moved her head to indicate the door. Rhonda got the idea and rose, Igor at her side. As she left the room the party swiftly broke up.

Just outside the dining hall, Elaine was waiting for her. "The king would like to see you in his study, Highness."

"Dammit, Elaine, stop it."

"Oh please, Ronni, let me."

"My god, you're actually enjoying this." The grinning girl just nodded her head eagerly. "Woman, you're having way too much fun at my expense. Igor, take her away and tend to that little errand for me."

"At once, Majesty."

"Listen you, don't you start. If you do I'll ..."

Igor grinned with mischief, caught her hand, and kissed that threatening finger. He winked at her. "King's waiting."

He was still chuckling as he led Elaine away, leaving Rhonda standing, staring at his retreating back. Finally she shook off the mood and hurried to the king's study. He looked up and smiled as she entered, indicating she should take a chair facing him. "Relax, girl, the formalities are over for a while."

She gave him an accusing look. "You've been planning this all along. Why didn't you warn me?"

"What? Give you a chance to run for your life?"

Rhonda shook her head with a laugh. "Dammit, Harald, that was embarrassing."

"Sorry. As you Americans say, my bad."

"Sorry? The hell you are, you're enjoying yourself."

"All right, you've got me there. Honestly, Ronni, the formal occasions will be few and far between, but they are important, vital even, to a monarchy. Gudrun or Ella can give you pointers on how it all works, as can Marlene or Torvil. This afternoon, I'll make the formal announcement, there'll be a bit of a ceremony, then it'll all be over."

"Oh, you're so full of it. It'll never be over. I'll spend eternity trying to be all formal and prissy, having no fun at all and ..."

His great roar of laughter stopped her, and she sat grinning at him. "So, you've had a taste of it already. Igor threw you in deep pretty quick.

Bran tells me this was something Igor was trying to set up all along anyway."

"Yeah, he saw his chance and threw me under the bus."

"Was it that bad, Ronni?"

"I was scared shitless, Harald. Good lord, I was expecting Igor to take command as he always does; have him tell me where to focus, then moving on that. Instead he put me in charge, then clammed up. He drove me crazy, wouldn't offer a damned thing or do anything until I gave him a direction."

Harald lost his smile. "I'd have thought Igor would be more of a help to you than that."

"Don't forget how he grew up, Sire. Igor believes that if you're going to be the alpha, then get busy and lead. He gave me the Gudrun case, then went off on poor old Illya, claimed the werewolves, then taught them the kneeling salute you and Sally described from her visions. He made me their queen, then stood back waiting for orders."

"Peter tells me you went full wolf with them."

"I know how the wolves work. I flew with the pack, hunted and located prey for them, then ate first meat while my alpha waited, showing submission. Yeah, he made me the Queen, and himself the grand alpha of both packs."

"You like it. Ronni, I know you well enough to know you did this for him and will hold to it forever. I do know how you feel, for I felt much the same way when Ella made me king."

"Wasn't your idea?"

"Oh hell no. I was more than content in my little antiques shop in England, trying to figure out just where I might find the delightful woman who haunted my dreams. Ella called us together, introduced me to Sally, then made me king and dared anyone to dispute it. Welcome to my world, Lady Hawk."

Her sweet laughter brought a smile to his face. "So you're telling me we're stuck with the jobs?"

"Afraid so, Ronni."

"You could abdicate."

"If I do you get the job."

"Oh no, don't you even dare think about that for another eight or nine thousand years."

His grin broadened, and he chuckled as she shook a finger at him, merriment dancing in her eyes. She saw it then. Harald had to be more careful with Sally, for their time together was short by his standards.

Torvil was his buddy, another man of a similar past to hang out with, but he'd never had children, and that was going to be her role, a daughter to tease, mentor, and dote on. Her own father had been a stern man and quite distant. She suddenly realized she needed this as much as he did. Rhonda returned his grin of mischief.

"So, tell me of the Russian sanctuary. Is it ready? Is it secure?" So began her full report on her adventures. She confessed her lack of judgment that sent the military to them and praised the way Peter and company had handled it. It was hours later when they emerged from that meeting, both smiling and chatting happily.

Their smiles faded quickly as they saw the look on Igor's face. "Igor, what is it?"

"Miss Gudrun has called for you, my Lady Hawk. She says Mr. Terry is in a bad way, the blade was poisoned."

"Son of a bitch," snarled Rhonda. "Where's Torvil?"

"Right here, Highness. How can I serve?"

"From classic Russian literature, if I wanted to poison a vampire what would I use?"

"Well, let me see, garlic is a standard myth, essence of a wild rose might be a possibility, wolf's bane maybe. Why do you ask?"

"Terry was wounded by a knife when he fought the vampire hunters. Justine and I patched him up but flew him off to Gudrun's special clinic anyway. He's had a turn for the worse. I'm willing to bet that bastard used a poisoned blade."

Her thumbs were flying on her phone as she spoke. A moment later her call was answered. "Gudrun here. Sorry I'm going to miss the party, Highness. I'll check in by satellite."

"Don't fret about that, honey, it's Terry I'm concerned for. Torvil says the best bets for these fools to use in trying to poison a vampire are garlic, essence of wild rose, or wolf's bane." Torvil spoke softly to her then she continued. "Deadly nightshade is another possibility."

"Got it, I'll pass that along. Oh, the doctor said he was patched up by a professional surgeon. Nice job little sister."

"Thanks. Go tend your guy, Gudrun." Rhonda broke the connection, a look of concern spoiling the smile on her lips.

She looked up to see Harald grinning at her. "What?"

"That was quick thinking, Ronni."

"Yeah, well, these bastards have been studying this crap for forty years. They would have ignored all the popular fluff and focused on the older, darker stuff. They're Russian, so Torvil would be our best bet for information."

"Damn that Bram Stoker anyway," muttered Ella.

"Enough of this," declared Harald. "Everyone go get ready for the gathering."

Rhonda arched an eyebrow at him. "Harald, just how formal is this going to be?"

"Wear clothes, no nudity." He chuckled as he walked away.

"Shit, he did it to me again, didn't he?"

Elaine came hurrying by. "Your clothes are already laid out on your bed, Highness." She smiled and hurried away.

Rhonda allowed Igor to take her arm and lead her up to their rooms where she found clothes for both of them laid out on the bed. She gasped with delight as she held up the bright blue gown. It was made of the finest linen, with long belled sleeves, and had bands of runes embroidered on the hem, neckline, and sleeves. The shoes were the softest leather and she groaned with delight as she slipped them on.

The gown fit her like a second skin, and she sighed with wonder as she admired herself in the mirror. Elaine came bustling in with a hairbrush in one hand and a gold circlet with a centered ruby in the other. "Hold still now while I fix your hair. I'll sneak a couple of hair pins in to hold the circlet in place for you."

Elaine fussed with Rhonda's hair for a few minutes then set the circlet in place. She produced a gold necklace with rubies, several gold bangles, and a number of rings from a jewelry box that Rhonda hadn't noticed.

"My god, Elaine, where did all this come from?"

"The gown is a gift from the Queen, and the jewels are from the king. They knew you came to us with only your feathers, and that you're more comfortable in a t-shirt and jeans, but you're a princess now. There will be the odd formal occasion, and you will need proper clothes. If you had bothered to look you would have seen that your closet has been fleshed out quite a bit."

"But this looks like something out of the middle ages ..."

Elaine laughed with delight. "It is, all of it. Well, the clothes were made by the costumer that makes the clothes for Torvil. She was utterly thrilled to get such a big order. Queen Sally declared that, since we're non-humans for the most part, the formal wear should reflect the styles of the day when Harald was first king."

"So, Sally didn't want to wear heels?"

Elaine giggled at that. "You know how she feels about heels."

"I do," chuckled Rhonda, "and gods bless her for it. This is so beautiful, and yet comfortable."

"Time to go," said Igor, as he emerged from the huge closet. He was dressed in loose linen pants, soft leather boots, with an embroidered tunic that was belted at the waist. He looked more like a Viking than a royal consort. Smiling, he took Rhonda's arm and led her back down toward the great hall.

Charles the butler stopped them just outside the door. The king saw his signal then rose to speak. As Harald rose to his feet, the room fell silent. Peeking into the room, Rhonda saw that every immortal except Gudrun was there, as were most of the human allies and a number of the werewolves, all the Lair's pack plus Nikka, Illya, and Anna from Russia.

Harald looked all around the hall, then spoke in a clear ringing voice that carried through the room and beyond. "My people, it's been only a few years now since we formed ourselves into an organized group. Since so many of us are quite elderly, we chose a monarchy such as we grew up in." This brought a round of chuckles.

"So far, we've done well. We've prospered, our numbers have grown, and now we must look to the future. A monarchy, by its very nature, requires a smooth succession from one monarch to the next for the sake and survival of the society. It's with this in mind, I've asked you all here today. At this time, I will now appoint my heir to the throne.

"This will ensure the continued prosperity of our combined people should the worst happen. With a capable heir in place, the kingdom will be secure. I've spent endless hours studying and consulting on this subject and have now made my decision.

"It is with the greatest of pleasure that I now proclaim Rhonda Stockman, better known to you as the Lady Hawk, my successor, my heir. Are there any objections?" There were none.

The king signaled, then Charles stepped into the room and announced Rhonda. "Announcing Lady Hawk, Queen of the Werewolves and her consort, the Grand Alpha, Igor."

As they walked in all the werewolves dropped to one knee and raised a fist high. "Hail the Queen. Hail Lady Hawk."

Rhonda made her way slowly to Harald's side, then signaled the wolves to rise. He turned to her and smiled. "Queen Lady Hawk, I now officially ask you to accept the position of my heir. As you know, a monarchy is usually passed from father to child, but I have no children. It is my intention to adopt you, will you accept this?"

She swallowed hard and blinked back the water forming in her eyes. This was way more than she'd expected. Slowly she nodded, cleared her throat, then knelt and spoke. "I accept, the post, the responsibility to our people, and I gladly accept the adoption."

Harald smiled with delight as he reached for her hand. "Rise my heir, my daughter, rise and greet your subjects. People, I present to you Her Royal Highness, Princess Lady Hawk, Queen of the Werewolves, Heir to the Throne."

While everyone was cheering Rhonda leaned close and whispered to Harald. "You sneaky beast, you didn't tell me you were going to do that."

"What, and give you a chance to run away?"

"I swear to you I'll do all in my power to live up to this and make you proud of me."

He smiled and winked at her. "I'm already quite proud of you. Speak to your people now, Princess."

She nodded and turned to the gathering, smiling brightly, and raised her arms. They fell silent to hear her. "My people, my friends, I swear to you, I'll do all in my power to protect you, to ensure you have good lives, and that you're kept safe to enjoy them.

"I will also confess, I told the king he wasn't allowed to abdicate for another ten thousand years, for as much as I love the idea of being a princess, I really don't want his job." This brought a round of laughter and applause. "Now I see by Tommy's waving arms over there, that the big screen has a message for us. Go ahead, Gudrun."

They all turned to the screen to see Gudrun's face, but she wasn't smiling. "My brothers and sisters, I'm pleased to tell you I fully support the king's decision here, and to say I believe he made the right one. I regret I'm not able to be with you today, but I am there in spirit.

"I also want to tell you I've just given myself a promotion and appointed myself to a new job. Since Ella, the greatest of us all, is the king's champion, I now promote myself to the position of the Lady Hawk's champion. You can all congratulate me later.

"Ah, I'm getting a signal from the hallway, and it comes with a smile. It appears my husband will survive, and we will soon return to you. With that I will now leave you to your celebration. Congratulations, Princess Lady Hawk, daughter of the king."

The screen went blank, and the king shook off the mood. "Well, it looks like good news from Europe. Since everyone is dressed for a party, let's clear away these chairs and get some music and dancing on the go."

The chairs were swiftly pushed back to the walls and medieval music filled the air. Harald took Sally's hand and led her in the dance. A few moments later Igor took Rhonda out onto the floor. "I'm sorry, my pretty bird, but we can't do the two-step to this. We'll go to the bar in the village one night soon for some of that." She laughed with delight as he twirled her around.

A Thief is Found

The party had lasted well into the night, and the sun was high in the sky when the king awakened to see his wife smiling brightly at him. He kissed her good morning, then rose easily from the bed to take his exercise in the training room. Dressed in his favorite leather armor, he stepped through the door and reached for his sword. Suddenly his hand froze as he noticed his saddle was missing.

With a roar of denial, Harald began to swear in three different languages. Sally came hurrying into the room with him. "Harald, Harald my love, whatever has happened?"

"By all the gods of treachery, Sally, we have a thief in the castle. My saddle's gone. When I get my hands on ..."

"Hush now, my lover, hush. Just give me a minute, I'll find it for you." She closed her eyes and drew three deep breaths, fighting to keep the grin of delight from her lips. After a moment she opened her eyes and grabbed him by the hand. "I know where it is, come on."

Leading him by the hand so he couldn't see the grin of mischief on her face, Sally led him through the castle and out the main doors. Harald stepped through the door to see his saddle atop a big red stallion. "What's going on here? Sally?"

"Hush now, my darling man, the Lady Hawk wants you."

Harald turned to see Rhonda gazing at him with her hands on her hips. "Well it's about time you surfaced. Come, Father, it's time for you to ride with hawk and hounds. Igor, Branimir." As she spoke both men transformed to wolf form and stood waiting beside the horse. With a piercing call she leaped into the air and climbed into the sky.

"You'll want this, my love." Sally grinned as she passed him a hawking glove. "Go on now, mount up before the horse goes to sleep."

With an ease his powerful stature would belie, the king leaped to the saddle and took the reins from Jillian. The hawk called again, and he held out his gloved fist as he looked up. A feathered missile dove toward him then suddenly spread her wings and alit lightly on his gloved hand. A grin of pure delight spread over his face as he leaned forward, and the horse raced away.

Out through the main gate he rode, holding the hawk on his fist. The slightest pressure of his knee gave the horse direction and it cantered along, head held high, the huge wolves pacing easily along beside. Herald swung his arm up and the hawk took flight, easily riding the air currents as she stayed out in front where he could see her.

Down through the fields they went until they reached and crossed the highway, then swung around for a trip along forest trails, then back to the highway and home through the fields on the other farm. The big horse easily leaped over the obstacles and fences. A slight touch of the reins slowed him as they returned to the main gates and trotted through. They reached the waiting people by the door and the king dismounted, held out his arm until the hawk returned to land on his gloved fist.

Herald was laughing with delight as the wolves and horse transformed and began pulling on clothes. "Transform, my daughter," he said, as he lowered his hand to the ground.

Rhonda gave a shriek of delight as she transformed and wrapped the dress Jill handed her about her slim form. "That was a barrel of fun."

"It was much more than that. You set this up, didn't you?"

"Got you back for the formal dinner." She was grinning, and he pulled her to him and hugged her gently. "So, forgive me for stealing your saddle?"

"By all the gods, Ronni, it's been centuries since I've ridden with hawk and hound. I can't thank you enough for this."

"You did that yesterday, father of mine. Now, I have another task for you."

Harald chuckled at that. "What do you need, Ronni. Whatever it is, I swear I'll make it happen."

"I've recently been informed that you and your bride never managed the time for a honeymoon. You pack your gear and git." Both Harald and Sally were staring at her, and her grin widened. "You heard me, get moving."

"Rhonda?"

"Sire, we have people settled into your castle in Germany, you've been talking about making the manor house in England a possible bolt hole or safe house, and you haven't yet seen the Russian Sanctuary. Things are quiet here at the moment. Take your lady fair on a slow tour of Europe, check out our sites there, and enjoy yourself."

Slowly a grin of mischief reached his lips. "So you really were after my job all this time."

Rhonda laughed heartily at that. "Yes I was, so get going and let me play."

"Yes, my daughter, I hear and obey." He smiled as he easily swept up his saddle and walked back inside.

Sally was hugging Rhonda tightly. "Gods, Ronni, I can't thank you enough for this. I've tried and tried to get him to take a few days off, but he won't."

"Does this mean I can call you Mom?"

"You do and I'll pluck your tail feathers." With a laugh of delight, Sally kissed Rhonda's cheek and hurried after her husband.

"That worked well," smiled Ella, as she stepped up beside Rhonda.

"Yeah, it did. He was really pleased. Now comes the hard part for you, Ella."

"Oh?"

"Yeah, you have to keep me from screwing things up while they're gone." Ella just smiled and patted her shoulder then walked back inside.

A Taste of the Big Chair

The next morning, King Harald and his bride boarded the plane and set out for England. Harald had sent messages to have his private suite prepared and even as the plane crossed a heaving ocean, the caretakers were busy.

Meanwhile, Rhonda sat in the king's favorite chair, a look of nervousness clouding her countenance. "Tommy."

"Yes, Highness?"

Rhonda sighed. "Et tu, Tommy?" He chuckled and spread his hands in a shrug, a grin of mischief playing at his lips. "You guys are having way too much fun at my expense."

"How does it feel in the big chair, Ronni?"

"Scary. If that damn computer systems beeps or buzzes I don't want to hear about it. Don't tell me anything, just deal with it."

"Yes, ma'am."

An hour later she was bored and left to find Torvil. She found him in the library with Ella, discussing her language idea.

For six days it was peaceful. Olla and Georg joined Igor's pack; Rhonda tried to spend time with everyone before they returned to their homes. On the seventh day it went all to hell. There had been a number of brutal underworld murders in New York, then Gina, the small but fierce vampire, arrived at the Lair, suitcase in hand. "I must speak with the king."

Gina was led into the great hall, then Elaine set about tracking down Rhonda. When they returned to the hall Gina gave a slight start, then knelt. "Highness, I must speak with the king."

Rhonda reached for her and raised her up. "Come, sit with me. Harald and Sally are away on their much-delayed honeymoon. You're stuck with me, I'm afraid."

"He left you in charge?"

"He did," said Ella, as she joined them.

At the stern look on Ella's face, Gina was instantly contrite. "Forgive me, Highness, I fear I'm a bit distraught. I ..."

"Easy now, tell me what happened."

"Yes, ma'am. As you know, I left Marco in New York and came to your adoption celebration alone. I knew having him around would upset the wolves and I didn't want to put a strain on the festivities."

"Understood and appreciated, Gina. Please go on."

Gina's back straightened and her eyes went hard as flint. "I returned home to find my Marco dead. I knew full well who had done this, so ..."

"You're the elusive hitman making headlines in New York these days?"

Gina sighed and let her shoulders slump. "Yes."

"Has justice been amply served?"

"Yes, it has, Highness."

"Good. Elaine can find you rooms. Hang out here with us for a few days until Gudrun gets back, then we'll put our heads together and see what the next move is. Actually, Agnes is a bit short-handed in Germany, does that have any appeal for you?"

"It does, Highness. I would like to return to Europe."

"All right, we have a plan. Give it a few days, then we'll send someone to pack up your apartment and get things in motion."

"Thank you, Highness. With your permission, I think I'll pay Amanda a visit too." Rhonda smiled and nodded then Gina backed away then turned and left the room.

Rhonda sighed and relaxed back in the chair, but she heard a beep then Tommy's soft mutter. "Crap. Talk to me Tommy."

"Something appears to be going on in San Francisco."

"Something strange in that neighborhood?"

Tommy chuckled. "Yes, ma'am. It's the sort of thing we usually look into."

"We're a bit short-handed until Gudrun and crew get back. Can it wait?"

"Well ..."

"Okay, who's available. Larise, isn't Frisco your hometown?"

"It is, Lady Hawk. Can I take Bran with me?"

"Time for the man to meet his mother-in-law?" Larise Parker just grinned, and Rhonda laughed. "Okay, Larise, go for it. Check it out, and if you need a vampire or another wolf, let me know."

As Larise fled in search of her husband to give him the news, Rhonda sighed and melted back into the big chair. "What is it, sweet Ronni? What troubles you?" asked Igor.

"It's Victor. He said he'd find that damned journal Johan kept, but I haven't heard a word from him. Johan said he gave it to a priest with instructions to take it to the Vatican. This has me messed up and I'll admit it."

"It's only been a few days, my pretty bird. Give the man time."

"Yeah, okay, I guess."

THE OLD PRIEST WRUNG his hands nervously then began to finger his rosary as he slowly descended the stairs. He'd been summoned to the Vatican by the head of a secret order, a man who no one seemed to know or want to. It was whispered that even the pope wouldn't go down into that office near the catacombs. This order had been hunting demons for centuries.

He finally reached the door and tapped gently. "Come." That voice was harsh, impatient, and filled with command.

With trembling hand, he turned the knob and entered, closing the door behind him. "Father Victor?"

"Yes, who are you and why are you here?"

"You sent for me, Father."

The man turned around to face him, then indicated he should sit. "So I did." He sank easily into the old wooden chair and faced the nervous priest. "It has come to my attention that you recently came into possession of a journal, the journal of a madman. Is this true?"

"It is, Father."

"How did you come by it?"

"A man came to my church and asked for confession. What he described to me was horrific. He gave me the journal and disappeared. I have not seen him since."

"Do you have it with you?"

"Yes." He pulled the journal out of the case he carried and passed it over.

The hard-faced man began to look through the pages. "Why did he give you this?"

"He asked that I keep it safe and deliver it into the hands of someone within the church who would be interested in its contents. I promised him I would."

"Did you give him absolution?"

"No, he asked that I not, for he believed himself beyond redemption."

"If half what I see here is true he may very well have been right."

"Is this something that interests you, Father Victor? Did I do right to bring it to you?"

"It is, and you did. I'm also pleased that you brought it to me in person and not trust the mails. I will study this, then place it in the sealed archives. Others of the order may peruse it from time to time under supervision. This is a thing of evil, written by an evil hand, and yet it may reveal more dark secrets than we now realize.

"Thank you, Father, you may go now with my blessing." The old priest rose, and with a short bow, hurried out and closed the door. He fairly ran back up the stairs in his haste to reach the sunlit streets of Rome.

Back in the office the harsh priest grinned as he sent a quick text then left the room through a secret door. He went down through the catacombs, out through a passage unused for centuries to the streets, then hailed a cab. Within a few hours he was in the air on his way back to Russia.

RHONDA GLANCED AT HER phone then broke into a bright smile. "It's Victor, he has the journal and will hold it in the sanctuary for me. The last loose end of that case is now tied off."

"Gudrun and Terry are on their way home," said Tommy. "They'll be here in a couple of hours."

Lady Hawk, Queen of the Werewolves, Heir to the Throne, sat back and smiled. Her first command mission was complete, a full success, and only one wounded man who was making a full recovery.

It was time for the heir to the throne to relax at last, but she couldn't, not completely. The visions of the Vampire Queen plus the knowledge that her time with her beloved Igor is finite, ever remain at the back of her mind. The Lady Hawk is all too aware of the fate that awaits her.

The End

Note from the author: And now, let us slip through time and space to another side of the galaxy and a time long past.

Rise of the Queen

by

Prudence MacLeod

Book one of the Elvish Chronicles
(second edition)
Copyright June / 2016

The Chronicles

Herein I will endeavor to record the events which brought the Elves back from the gates of extinction to rule the vast forests of Elendor. Through several twists of fate, and the rediscovery of their ancient magics they were returned, and now they inhabit and control the vast forests of northern Elendor.

It all began with the sudden appearance of the assassin...

Shadow Assassin

In the city of Magdan, as ruled by the Geni Overlord, Ocra, the night had fallen strangely silent. It was one of those odd silences that sometimes falls for no reason, and vanishes a moment later. However, it was enough. Ariel, newly promoted to the City Watch, arose from her bed with liquid grace, stepping into her soft boots and silently sliding her sword from the scabbard hanging at her bedside.

Ariel, descended from the High Born Elves of Elendor, had managed to earn her freedom from slavery and rise to a post in the Watch. Few Elves ever managed to earn freedom; none had ever been trusted to carry a sword.

With silent steps she slipped from the building and cast her gaze about for anything that was amiss. She found it on the rooftop, a shadow in the moonlight that did not belong. A few swift and silent strides carried Ariel to the dark figure. "Stand and surrender." She spoke in a clear ringing voice as she laid the tip of her blade against the intruder's neck.

"Not tonight, little sister. Go back to your warm bed and your dreams of glory. Live to fight another day." Ariel was shocked. First, the voice was low pitched, yet feminine, and gentle, almost loving, caressing her senses. Second, the intruder had spoken in High Elvish, a language that was forbidden on pain of death. Few remained who could actually speak it.

Ariel didn't realize the figure had moved until a strong arm encircled her neck and a silvery blade caressed her cheek. Again that gentle loving voice spoke. "Go back, little sister. I've come here this night to take a life; I'd prefer it not be yours. Return to your warm bed and sweet dreams." The arm left her neck and a strong hand deftly relieved her of the sword. She barely noticed it happen.

Ariel felt the intruder step away and she turned to face her opponent. The moon broke from behind a cloud to show her a tall Elf with elaborate tattoos on her left cheek. Ariel swallowed and stepped back. "You're one of the ancient Borni tribe. You can't be real. Your people died out centuries ago."

The woman's eyes danced with merriment and her smile was radiant. "No, little sister, we did not vanish from the realms, but we did withdraw from this one for a time. Now we're returning." That voice was still soft and gentle, almost hypnotic. "I must be about the business now. I beg you, do not follow me or sound the alarm. It would grieve me to have to harm you."

The woman tossed Ariel her sword, then leaped from the roof top to vanish into the shadows of an alley below.

Without a second thought, Ariel followed as best she could. This Borni was like a wisp of smoke in the breeze. Somehow Ariel managed to catch sight of her quarry often enough to keep up yet stay back out of sight.

Her heart froze in her chest, the woman had slipped into Ocra's house, the most heavily guarded palace in the entire region.

Ariel knew she should sound the alarm. She knew it would mean her death if it was discovered that she had known of the intruder but done nothing. She swallowed hard, but before she could make a decision, the Borni slipped out of the house, carrying a sack. There had been no alarm.

"A common thief," mused Ariel, disappointed, and not knowing why. And then she saw the blood dripping from the bag. The Borni had said she'd come to take a life. By all the gods, what had she done? Ariel followed as the assassin headed for the wall that surrounded the town. With a cat-like grace the woman leaped to the top and disappeared over it, vanishing into the darkness below.

Ariel climbed swiftly to the wall and peered over as well. The assassin was sitting on a horse below, waiting for her with a huge smile. "Well? Are you coming or not?"

Without a second thought, Ariel slipped over the wall and landed beside the horse. A hand was extended and she grabbed it, swinging up behind the Borni as the horse leaped away. She could hear the alarm sounding back in the town.

As she clung to the rider, Ariel's heart beat wildly with the sudden and intoxicating rush of true freedom.

Don't miss out!

Visit the website below and you can sign up to receive emails whenever Prudence MacLeod publishes a new book. There's no charge and no obligation.

https://books2read.com/r/B-A-ZKBBB-SUVYC

BOOKS 2 READ

Connecting independent readers to independent writers.

Also by Prudence MacLeod

Children of the Goddess
Lady Blue
Fallen Angel
Lady Justice
Lady Shadow
Lady Seeker
Watcher and Warrior
Shadow Ascending

Children of the Wild
Immortal Tigress
Children of the Wolf
Vampire's Lair
The Hawk and the Wolf
The Oregon Incident
Race the Wind
Heir to the Throne

Forgotten Worlds
Suvi

Echo of the Past
Survivors
Ship
Fleet
Unite
IGEN
T.E.N.

Nova series
Novan Witch
Assassin of Nova
Beyond Nova
Claimstake
Red Nova

Watch for more at https://www.prudencemacleod.com/.

Telling a story is like knitting a sweater. Start with a ball of possibilities, pull out one small thread and begin. With luck and patience you will create something quite wonderful.

About the Author

On a far off windswept island Jennifer Crandall sits with her dogs and cats creating fantastic stories for all to enjoy. She publishes as JL Crandall, Prudence MacLeod, and Jenni Leigh.

Read more at https://www.prudencemacleod.com/.